"I need to ask a

"Well, I hope it's a simp— —— ——— —— ——
filled your dance card by asking me to go to
prison."

"You know how important all this is," Brognola
continued. "This investigation has gone on for
years. We're probably just weeks away from
handing down major indictments. Striker, I—"

"Wait a minute," Bolan interrupted. "I've wanted to
kill that swaggering bastard every minute of the
past two weeks. I understand that you want to
prosecute and need the Giancarlos for your case,
but I don't want anything to do with it. Witness
protection at this level goes against everything I
believe in."

"Striker, with the cooperation of the Giancarlos, we
can dig out the rest of them, wipe out the whole
Chicago Mob. By keeping the Giancarlos alive, we
can do more good with this one investigation than
you've ever done with your guns. Doesn't that
mean anything?"

Bolan sighed tiredly and leaned down to pull a
leather bag from under the seat. Inside was the
combat harness containing Big Thunder.

"Okay. But we do it my way."

MACK BOLAN®

The Executioner

DON PENDLETON's EXECUTIONER

MACK BOLAN®

The Killing Urge

A GOLD EAGLE BOOK FROM

WORLDWIDE®

TORONTO · NEW YORK · LONDON · PARIS
AMSTERDAM · STOCKHOLM · HAMBURG
ATHENS · MILAN · TOKYO · SYDNEY

First edition August 1988

ISBN 0-373-61116-1

Special thanks and acknowledgment to
Mike McQuay for his contribution to this work.

Printed in U.S.A.

What do we mean by patriotism in the context of our times? . . . A patriotism that puts country ahead of self; a patriotism which is not short, frenzied outbursts of emotion but the . . . steady dedication of a lifetime.

—Adlai Stevenson, August 27, 1952

Crime is the darkness that tries to extinguish the light of civilization. I've dedicated my life to keeping the flame burning.

—Mack Bolan

THE
MACK BOLAN®
LEGEND

Nothing less than a war could have fashioned the destiny of the man called Mack Bolan. Bolan earned the Executioner title in the jungle hell of Vietnam.

But this soldier also wore another name—Sergeant Mercy. He was so tagged because of the compassion he showed to wounded comrades-in-arms and Vietnamese civilians.

Mack Bolan's second tour of duty ended prematurely when he was given emergency leave to return home and bury his family, victims of the Mob. Then he declared a one-man war against the Mafia.

He confronted the Families head-on from coast to coast, and soon a hope of victory began to appear. But Bolan had broken society's every rule. That same society started gunning for this elusive warrior—to no avail.

So Bolan was offered amnesty to work within the system against terrorism. This time, as an employee of Uncle Sam, Bolan became Colonel John Phoenix. With a command center at Stony Man Farm in Virginia, he and his new allies—Able Team and Phoenix Force—waged relentless war on a new adversary: the KGB.

But when his one true love, April Rose, died at the hands of the Soviet terror machine, Bolan severed all ties with Establishment authority.

Now, after a lengthy lone-wolf struggle and much soul-searching, the Executioner has agreed to enter an "arm's-length" alliance with his government once more, reserving the right to pursue personal missions in his Everlasting War.

Prologue

Vic D'matto played the flashlight over his new white silk suit and white shoes, grunting at the blood that had spattered liberally all over himself and the small deckmate's cabin of the fifty-foot yacht.

He turned the glare of the light on the face of his brother-in-law, Tony, and wished again that Angela had let him find her a nice husband in Sicily before going to the old man with this white trash Neapolitan. Wasn't a smart one in the bunch. Not a one.

"You stupid son of a bitch," he hissed. "Look what you've done to my new suit. How the hell am I supposed to clean blood off of silk?"

"Whydya blame me?" Tony said, holding up the claw hammer. "Is it my fault that the jerk wouldn't die?"

A small stream of blood ran off the grooves of the hammer, dripping on D'matto's pant leg. "Damn! You did it again!" he said, and grabbed the hammer out of Tony's hand. "I ought to take this damn thing to your head!"

"C'mon, Vic. Cut me some slack."

"Aaah, hell, *paesano*." He reached out and cuffed the kid playfully on the cheek. "But you've got to replace the suit."

"Sure, Vic."

D'matto played the light on the corpse of the big Cuban, which lay on the floor beside the bunk they were sitting on. He'd been a tough kill, all right, all muscle and no brains to bash out.

He kicked the body once more for good measure, then turned around in the bunk to open the porthole. The thing didn't open like a regular window, but he figured it out quick enough and opened it to a blast of salt air and a vision of the Biscayne Island moorings where the boat was tied up, the lights of Miami twinkling enticingly in the distance. Vic sure wished he hadn't been sent down here with Ferrari. He'd love to spend some time trying to get to know a few rich Miami beach broads, but he'd be damned if he'd give his sister's husband any ideas on that subject.

"Man, I wish this damn thing would stop moving," Tony said, a hand to his stomach.

"It's a boat, stupid," Vic said, shoving the claw hammer out the porthole to slip into the dark, churning water, "it's supposed to move."

"Tell my stomach that."

"I told you to lay off the linguine," Vic returned, his attention directed to movement along the Venetian Causeway that connected the mainland with Miami Beach by way of the islands. "But you wouldn't listen."

"It's not the linguine, it's this damned boat."

"Shh," Vic said. "I think somebody's coming."

He looked down the long dock full of power boats covered with canvas, and watched a white Cadillac exit the causeway and pull up near the end of the dock. "Looks like Jughead's traveling in style," he said.

Tony turned and got up next to Vic, both men taking turns shoving each other out of the way to look through the port. Vic heard the sound of laughter first, then watched Enrico "Jughead" Pallonatti slide his large bulk out from behind the wheel of the Coupe Deville, followed by two young women, a redhead and a blonde, both dressed for the streets.

"Oh, man," Tony said. "Lookit them broads!"

Vic slapped him. "Would you stop with the broads?" he said. "I don't want to have to make a widow out of my sister."

"Hey, I was just lookin'."

"Don't look. It's bad for you. C'mon. Help me stow this meat, would you?"

As Jughead and the prostitutes made their way down the long pier, Vic and Tony got down on the floor and shoved the Cuban under his bunk, having to drape the spread down to cover him. The old man had waited a long time to repay the insults the Giancarlo family had heaped upon him, and now the payback would begin.

"Hey!" came Pallonatti's voice from the pier. "Jorge!"

"Do we take him now?" Tony asked.

"No," Vic answered. "Let's wait and see if he takes it out where it's quieter. We'll hide in the galley."

"The what?"

Vic shone the flashlight in Tony's face again. "The kitchen," he said. "The kitchen."

"Well, jeez. Why didn't you say so?"

As they made their way out of the cabin and down the dark, narrow hallway toward the galley, they could hear the women giggling as Pallonatti helped them on deck.

"I told that son of a bitch I wanted to take it out tonight," came Jughead's muffled voice. "He's probably laying off drunk someplace."

Vic led Tony through the narrow, short door and into the galley, enough light spilling into the room from the marina for them to move around. The galley was small but fancy, all polished wood and stainless steel. As Tony moved to hide in the pantry, Vic picked up a large cleaver from a butcher-block table and joined him.

"Here," he said, handing the heavy knife to Tony, "hang on to this." He squeezed into the pantry with his brother-in-law and half closed the louvered door. The smell of spices was strong in the confined space.

"Is he gonna be carryin' heat?" Tony asked as he swished the cleaver around, playing with it.

"Jughead always carried a .38 in his back pocket and a box knife in his sock," Vic said, pushing Tony's arm aside. "And watch out for him. He's rough for an old fart."

"Jorge!" came Pallonatti's voice from the hall. "Albert's boat is real nice, but he sure needs to get him a crew he can trust."

"Do we need him to take out the boat, Pally?" asked a female voice.

"Pally?" Tony stifled a laugh.

"Would you shut up?" Vic whispered.

The other woman spoke. "Maybe it's better this way. More cozy."

"Sure," Jughead said. "You girls can be my crew. Why don't you cast off the lines and I'll get us outta the slip."

Their voices retreated back down the hallway. Vic and Tony came out of the pantry, Tony still holding his stomach. "God, this rocking."

"It's going to get worse," Vic said. "I think he's going to take us out in the ocean. Hey, look."

A pair of female legs without shoes moved past the galley port, hurrying to cast off as the sound of the engine sputtering to life rattled the pans on the wall.

Within minutes they were under way, Vic keeping an eye out the porthole, watching the marina and the lights of Miami fade out of sight. He was itching to get this taken care of and get back to dry land. The movement of the boat wasn't doing his stomach any good either, though he'd never admit that to Tony. His ancestors had been fishermen, but it sure didn't seem to be in *his* blood.

Another five minutes passed and the boat's engine died. Vic smiled. Jughead, the big sailor, was probably afraid of getting too far away from land. On the other hand, he probably had other things to occupy his mind.

Vic turned to Tony. "Let's do it," he said.

The younger man's eyes glowed in the darkness. "Yeah," he said eagerly, holding up the cleaver.

Vic reached into the waistband of his ruined pants and pulled out the nickel-plated .45. He snapped a load into the chamber and cautiously pushed open the small door, moving out into the dark, empty hallway.

The two men moved slowly, cautiously down the hall, pausing at the short flight of steps that led up to the main deck. "I got Jughead," Vic said. "You make sure the broads don't do anything crazy."

Tony nodded, licking dry lips. It bothered Vic somewhat that the kid liked this part of it so much. It was business, after all, not fun.

Slowly, carefully, he moved up the stairs to the push-open double doors at the top. Staying low, he used the barrel of the .45 to shove one of the doors open a crack. Jughead was sprawled on a lounge chair, the redhead, naked except for black bikini panties, on top of him, kissing his balding head. He looked ridiculous, an old man trying to appear young, with an open shirt and gold chains all tangled up with his gray chest hair. Vic shook his head and spit on the stairs. The blonde, dressed in a black leather miniskirt, sat on cushions beside the couple, snorting cocaine out of a small gold box.

Vic turned to Tony and gave him the thumbs-up sign. "Piece of cake," he whispered, then motioned Tony forward.

Slowly Vic walked through the doorway, the people on deck too wrapped up in themselves to even notice.

Tony followed him through, a big smile splitting his face when he saw Jughead.

"Big night, huh, capo?" Vic said.

In a flash, Pallonatti shoved the startled redhead at the two men and rolled to a sitting position, his hand going for his back pocket. Vic pushed past the woman, to stick the .45 right in the man's face. "Don't do it," he said low.

"Who's that?" Jughead asked. "Vic? Vic D'matto?"

"Let's have the piece, capo," Vic said, pulling back the hammer.

"Hey, sure, Vic. Sure." Gingerly the man stood up and pulled the short-barrel .38 out of his back pocket, held it out with two fingers. "What's the problem?"

"Over the side." Vic looked at the gun. "We got some things to talk over."

Pallonatti tossed the gun over his shoulder to splash into the ocean. The night was beautiful, star-filled, the skyline of Miami just a glimmer in the distance. He sat up slowly. "You sure put a scare into—"

"The box knife, too," Vic said.

Tony had moved the women to the corner of the deck and was eyeing the redhead, sweet-talking her.

Jughead got out the box knife, and the sheathed razor blade followed the revolver into the Atlantic.

"Good, capo." Vic backed several feet away and turned to Tony. "Help the broads take a swim."

"What?" Tony asked. "Can't we—"

"Don't even say it," Vic replied, "or you'll be taking a swim with them."

"You heard the man," Tony told the women. "Over the side."

The blonde protested. "Please, no... it's too far to..."

Tony picked her up and threw her overboard. The redhead grabbed a seat cushion life jacket and jumped in after her.

"What's this 'capo' shit?" Pallonatti asked, reclaiming his lounger. "That was a long time ago."

"Not to the old man," Vic said. "Not to Rocco."

"Hey look," the man returned. "I'm sorry about all that, but it was just business, you know. Past and gone." He tried to stand. Tony rushed over to push him back down.

"You're fish food, old man," he said.

"Who's the kid?" Jughead asked.

"Nice place for a vacation, isn't it?" Vic commented. "Did the government take such good care of you that you can afford this?"

"Albert told you I was down here, didn't he?" Jughead asked.

"Albert works with us now," Tony said, beaming.

"You talk too much," Vic told him, then turned back to the old man. "You seen your boss lately?"

"Look, Vic," Pallonatti said, sitting forward and opening his arms wide. "None of us wanted to turn government, but they had so much on us—"

"That you decided to burn the Villanis to save your own necks." Vic pulled up a deck chair in front of Pallonatti and sat down. The man was a cool number, his eyes hard and watchful. Not a bit of the coward in him. Well, they'd see. "This thing of ours, this *cosa nostra*, it don't forget. The ties are blood, and can only be met with blood."

"Save it for the old ladies, dago," Jughead said. "I don't give a fu—"

Vic jumped up and slashed him viciously across the face with the barrel of the .45, knocking him back on the lounger. Blood ran freely from Pallonatti's mouth and nose. "I've got four names for you," Vic said as he sat down again. "I want you to tell me where they're living."

"Look . . . Vic," Jughead said, spitting out a tooth. "The government, they set us all up with different names, different lives. None of us know where the others are. We don't even know what their new names are."

"The worse for you." Vic nodded to Tony, who grabbed Pallonatti's right hand and pulled it up onto the deck rail. "I'm going to ask you each name, and if you don't tell me where the guy is, you'll lose a finger. Another name, another finger."

"I don't know anything, Vic," Pallonatti whined. "Honest to God. I swear on my mother's grave."

"Your mother's still alive," Vic stated grimly. "Okay, first, Vito Perezzi."

"Vic, I don't know, I— Aaah!"

With a solid thunk on the wood rail, the cleaver had severed the little finger, which dropped onto the deck.

"God, Vic . . . Jesus, I swear to you . . ."

"Second name, Mario Ottoni . . . mouthpiece, huh?"

Jughead's face was strained, tears streaming from his eyes. "I don't..."

Thunk.

Another finger hit the deck. Jughead's scream shattered the night.

"Next name, Stinky Barberi."

Pallonatti was swooning now, moaning. He didn't speak.

Vic nodded to Tony. The heavy blade fell and the man's middle finger dropped clean.

Vic crouched to bring his mouth close to the other man's ear. "Now, here's the big one, Jughead. It's stupid for you to protect them. Tell me where the old man is. Where's Giancarlo... where's Old Sam?"

Pallonatti stared at him with deep, pain-filled eyes, but said nothing. Vic shrugged and stood up. "Oh well, I guess you'll never play the piano again."

Tony laughed loudly as he gleefully hacked off the index finger. He let go of Pallonatti, who pulled the bloody stump of his hand to his chest, hugging it.

"Go find me some rope," Vic told Tony. He turned back to Jughead. "C'mon, capo, let's go on upstairs."

He forced the man to his feet and up the ladder leading to the small wheelhouse on the upper deck. A motorized dinghy was suspended by ropes near the ladder. Vic stopped to examine the little boat before following Pallonatti.

"God, it's a great night, isn't it?" he remarked as he breathed in the salt air. "Swell yacht, too. Albert's doing okay for himself."

"Get it over with," Jughead wailed. He was doubled over, still cradling the remnants of his hand. It was dripping blood into a small puddle on the deck. "Please. We were friends once . . . just do me."

"Well we're still friends, aren't we? Like you said, this is just business."

"Please, Vic . . ."

"Here's the rope!" Tony called, starting up the ladder.

Vic waved him up. "Tie our buddy to the helm, Tony."

"The what?"

"The steering wheel, stupid. Don't you know anything?"

"I ain't never been on no freakin' boat before," Tony said, pouting as he lashed the whimpering Pallonatti to the helm. "Why you always gotta make fun of me?"

"Aaah, you're too sensitive," Vic replied, shoving his gun back into his waistband. "When you get done there, go down into the engine room and see if you can figure out some way to punch a hole in the bottom of this thing. I'll be working on getting that little dinghy down into the water."

"Sure." Tony disappeared below.

Vic descended the ladder. The old man wasn't going to be happy that Jughead didn't know anything, but at least they were taking care of the capo. He could only do what he could do. He snapped the clamps off the line attached to the dinghy and slowly lowered it into the water, then reclamped the rope until they were ready to leave the yacht.

When he was done, he leaned against the rail and lit a cigarette, listening with half an ear to Jughead's pleas in case he came up with something. The breeze was warm, the night peaceful. When he'd left Chicago that morning it had been twenty-eight degrees. It was a shame there wasn't something else for him to do down here in Florida, even though Tony was like a stone around his neck.

He stared down at his suit, frowning at the blood stains, then went belowdecks. He found a suit in Pallonatti's cabin and changed into it. It was much too big, but at least it wouldn't get him arrested. Quickly he rifled the cabin, pocketing several thousand in cash. After satisfying himself that there was nothing left worth taking, he went back up on deck and lit another cigarette.

The kid came charging up the ladder minutes later, stumbling onto the deck, his pants wet to the knees. "Oh man!" he yelled. "I pried some boards loose and the whole damned ocean started to pour in. Let's get the hell out!"

Vic tossed his butt over the side to sizzle in the dark waters, then climbed into the dinghy. Tony hurried in, too, rocking the little boat and nearly capsizing it.

The motor started easily. As they putted off toward the Miami shore a couple of miles in the distance, the yacht was already riding low in the water. They passed the redhead clinging desperately to her life preserver, their wake nearly taking her under.

Vic turned back once to look at the yacht. It was submerged except for the upper deck and part of the prow, tilted crazily at a forty-five-degree angle. Jughead's big, white-shirted belly stood out like a medicine ball under the bright quarter moon. In another few minutes everything had sunk.

True to his fears, Tony's upset stomach finally got the better of him. As Tony heaved over the side, Vic looked with disdain at Pallonatti's ugly, baggy suit. "That reminds me," he said. "As soon as we call the old man, you're replacing the suit you ruined."

BENITO VILLANI sat at the table in his small kitchen, a cigarette stuck between his fingers, the phone to his ear. It was the news he'd been afraid he'd hear. "Yeah, Vic...yeah. I understand. There wasn't anything you could do."

A bottle of Chianti stood on the table, halfful tumblers set before Villani and the man who sat across from him. The room smelled of garlic and baking bread. In a small alcove in the wall was a statue of the Virgin Mary, and a picture of Pope Pius XII blessing a much younger Villani hung in a cracked frame.

"No...I don't want you hangin' around down there," Villani said, taking a small sip of wine, drawing it out, savoring the one glass a day he was allowed. "You get a plane back in the morning. I got more work for you. Yeah, Vic. You done just fine. *Ciao.*"

He hung up the phone slowly and looked at the man across from him. "You was right. Jughead, he didn't know nothin'."

"I can guarantee you the bodies of the other four," the man said.

Villani stared at him thoughtfully for a minute. "Even Old Sam?"

"Especially Old Sam. Do we have a deal?"

"You offer me salvation," Villani said. "My Rocco's in Joliet for a hundred and fifty years. Ricci's dead. Tomas...dead. I've outlived everybody and I got nobody to take care of the family business."

"You've got me."

"You fill my vendetta. You take care of these traitors to the blood and what's mine is yours." Villani finished his wine. "The other families will pay, too. They stand to lose just as much as me. I'm old and tired, but I still got some power. It's yours just as soon as I see that Old Sam is livin' with the fishes."

The man grabbed Ben Villani's brown withered hand and brought it to his lips, kissed it. "I swear to you on my life that your vendetta will be carried out."

The old man's lower lip began to quiver. Tears came to his eyes, but did not fall. "My boy," he said. "My boy."

Mack Bolan sat watching Rocco Villani's muscled back rising and falling as the man counted out push-ups on the concrete floor of his cell.

"Ninety-three... ninety-four... ninety-five..."

Rocco was soaked with sweat, his biceps bunching up in small spasms with the effort. Bolan thought that if he had to live through this daily ritual many more times, he'd go insane.

"Ninety-six... ninety-seven..."

It was always the same, a hundred push-ups, then the posturing, then the boasting. Prison seemed to agree with the hood. He was around people he knew and understood, and his routine wasn't much different than it was on the outside—screw who you could, when you could, for whatever reason you could think of. It was Rocco Villani's idea of what life was supposed to be.

"Ninety-eight... ninety-nine... a hundred!"

The man jumped to his feet and hurried to the full-length mirror he'd installed at the back of the cell. He wanted to pose while his muscles were still tensed up.

"Yeah," he said with self-satisfaction, sliding from one imagined weight lifter's pose to the next. "Hard as a rock...that's the kid. Look, Belasko. Better than yesterday, right?"

"They broke the mold when they made you," Bolan replied, answering to his alias, Mike Belasko.

"You bet they did." Villani put his hands behind his head to make the muscles ripple. "I'll bet you I'm the toughest son of a bitch they got in this place. This damned hole's all mine and everybody knows it, too. Don't they?"

"They know it," Bolan said mechanically.

"Damn right they do," Villani said, walking back to his bunk to pick up a towel. He draped it over his shoulders and sat down, facing Bolan. "Yeah, the kid's still got it, the body of a twenty-year-old. You want to get a feel of one of these muscles?"

He offered an arm, but Bolan declined. "I'll take your word for it, Rocco."

The man made a face. "You're an odd one, Belasko, you know that?" he asked, not expecting an answer. "But I saw you taking care of yourself out in the yard and I know you've got guts. Old Rocco doesn't miss anything. I'm as sharp as a tack. You know how to keep your trap shut, too."

"Good way of staying out of trouble," Bolan replied.

Villani used the towel on his hair, fluffing it into a tangled mess that hung all over his face. "You know, I can use a man that knows how to keep his mouth shut and can take care of himself."

"Well, I hope you find one." Bolan stretched out on the bunk. He stared through the bars, watching other men in cages across the expanse of open courtyard of C Block. He was all tensed up inside, and he couldn't handle this much longer. How had he let himself get talked into this mess?

"You're a funny man," Villani said, snorting. "You know, I'm not going to be in here forever. When I get out, I'll be taking over the family business, if you know what I mean?"

"The only way you'll ever get out of here is with a can opener," Bolan answered. "Besides, I'm just here to get screwed in court with some more charges. Soon as that's over, I'm back at Folsom."

Villani got off his bunk to stare with dark eyes down at Bolan. "You don't get it, tough guy. My family'll never let me rot in here. We're connected. Hell, my pop lives about fifteen miles from here. He's not going to let me rot."

"From what I hear, your family's all busted up now, thanks to Old Sam."

Rocco spit loudly on the floor. "My pop's already taken care of Old Sam's capo," he said proudly. "And he'll get the rest of 'em, too. Then he'll spring me out of here...."

"How'd he manage that?" Bolan asked, sitting up and sliding his legs off the bed. "I heard all those guys were on witness protection."

"My pop's the best, Belasko," Villani said. Catching his reflection in the mirror, he began posturing again. "He came up with Luciano back in the old days. He can do anything."

Bolan stood and walked to the bars, grabbing the uncompromising metal. The time between supper and lights out was always the worst—cage time, he called it. He felt like an animal locked up with other animals. He watched a guard climbing the metal steps on the other side of the courtyard, then moving along the catwalk in their general direction. This was as good an opportunity as any. "Your pop's a liar. He can't crack witness protection," he told Villani. "Nobody can."

With angry strides Rocco crossed the cell to pull Bolan off the bars, but the big man slipped away from him. "Damn you!" Villani spit. "Don't say nothing bad about my pop. If I say he can crack witness protection, then he can do it."

"All right," Bolan said. "How?"

"I don't need to tell you nothing!"

"Because you know nothing," Bolan needled him. "You're just another cheap hood with a big mouth."

Rocco lunged at him, his oxlike face twisted in rage. Bolan sidestepped him, grabbing him by the hair and slamming him hard into his mirror. It smashed, the glass falling out in huge shards. Hurrying to the bars, Bolan turned and crouched, waiting.

Villani shook his head dumbly, blood flowing from a cut on the crown. He picked up a large sliver of glass and moved slowly forward.

"Hey!" Bolan called. "Hey! This clown's gone nuts in here!"

Rocco charged, swinging out with the glass. Bolan ducked, then came up hard with a fist in the man's gut. To no avail—the push-ups had been doing their job.

"That's it!" came a voice from outside the bars, the guard, whom Bolan had seen earlier. "Move to opposite sides of the cell, right now!"

The man had removed his billy club and was reaching for his pass key.

"Screw you!" Rocco yelled, swinging out again.

This time Bolan grabbed the hand holding the glass and slammed it against the iron bar. Rocco used his other hand to pull savagely on Bolan's hair.

The guard was blowing his whistle, the other prisoners yelling and applauding, as Bolan came around hard with both fists. He clipped Rocco viciously on the side of the head, driving him back.

Before Villani could charge again, the door of the cell swung open. Several guards in uniform charged in, surrounding Bolan and knocked him to the floor. They cuffed his hands behind his back.

"You son of a bitch!" Rocco screamed. The two of them were dragged to their feet and out into the courtyard.

The captain of the guard, a gaunt man with a pale death's-head face, stood outside the cell, his hands behind his back and his jaw muscles working overtime. "Take them both to solitary," he ordered as the other inmates cheered loudly.

But Bolan wasn't taken to solitary. Both he and Rocco were dragged downstairs, but Rocco continued down the long hallway to solitary by himself. The guard captain put out a hand to stop Bolan before he could enter the bars to that block. "Take him to the warden," he told the guards escorting Bolan.

They led him off the other way then, outside the cell block and across the yard to the executive offices, where he was deposited unceremoniously in front of a door marked: Justin Tremaine, Director. The warden.

One of the two guards who held him by the arms knocked lightly on the door. Tremaine himself came to answer it.

"This is the one you wanted," the guard said. "We had to break him out of a fight with one of the other prisoners to get him here."

"Thank you," Warden Tremaine said, opening his door wide. "You can leave him with me."

"Watch this one," the guard said. "He's a trouble-maker deluxe."

"Take the cuffs off him." The guards protested but did as they were told.

Warden Tremaine ushered Bolan into his office. It was small, with everything neat and in its place. Strictly business, with no clutter, no warmth anywhere. Another man was standing with his back to the room, staring out the large window that faced onto the yard and the famous high cement walls that surrounded Joliet.

"Thanks," Bolan said as he tried to rub some feeling back into his wrists. "They cut off my circulation."

"A troublemaker deluxe," the man at the window said, chuckling. Then he turned around.

"Hal!" Bolan said. "I was beginning to think you decided to leave me here."

Hal Brognola crossed the room and embraced Bolan warmly, but the Executioner was slow to return the warmth. Brognola pulled back and looked at him through narrowed eyes. "You okay?"

"I'm not going back in there," Bolan said without preamble, "so don't ask."

"That rough?"

Bolan shook it off. "I can take care of myself, you know that. It was more...sickening than anything."

As if in response to his words, Warden Tremaine picked up a white paper bag from his desk and tossed it to Bolan.

"Put those on while you tell me about it," Brognola said.

The bag contained Bolan's clothes, the most welcome sight the big man had seen in quite some time. He quickly stripped off his blue cotton shirt and prison jeans and began getting into his own stuff. He'd have rather had a hot shower first, but he'd take what he could get.

"Anything from Rocco?" Brognola asked.

"Nothing he didn't fantasize," Bolan answered, pulling into a pair of slacks. "I came at it from fifty different angles, from friendship to confrontation, but I never got any farther than Rocco's insistence that his old man put the hit on Pallonatti. If Old Sam has cracked witness protection, Rocco doesn't know about it."

He picked the bright knit shirt out of his bag and slipped it over his head.

"Could he have just been playing it close to the vest?" Brognola asked.

"Absolutely not."

"You seem so positive."

Bolan nodded to the small washroom just off the office. "You mind?" he asked the warden, pointing to the taps.

"Be my guest."

Bolan turned on the taps and began washing his hands, talking to the big Fed through the open doorway. "Rocco's just a dumb ox, Hal," he said. "His idea of an intellectual pursuit is trying to figure out how to turn on the television in the rec room. I figure his father didn't get to be where he is without having a few smarts of his own, so I don't think he'd trust Rocco with any important information."

"Did you get anything else out of him?"

Bolan splashed his face, then dried off. "Yeah. For what it's worth, I do believe him, that Old Sam engineered the hit. But I think it might have been blind luck. You know, somebody accidentally spotted Jughead or something. He broke his own cover. Any leads on the body yet?"

"We're not sure," Brognola replied. "We traced him from his new home in Denver to Miami Beach, but there we lost the trail. Last week the bodies of a couple of prostitutes washed up on the beach in south

Miami, and friends of theirs said they left one night about the same time Jughead disappeared, saying they were going boating with a 'sugar daddy.' We're still checking that out.''

Bolan pulled a light jacket out of the bag of personal effects and slipped it on. Tremaine handed him another package containing his pocket change, wallet and wristwatch.

"Come on, Hal, let's get out of here. I want to get some real food.'' Bolan opened his wallet and checked its contents. "Your treat.''

THE WAITRESS SET a rib-eye steak in front of Bolan. It crowded the two cheeseburgers and the club sandwich that were already there. Then the woman went away, shaking her head.

Brognola scooted sideways in the diner booth and put a leg up on the upholstered bench. "She sure is looking at you funny.''

Bolan nodded, cutting into the steak. "In addition to the obvious—'' he pointed to the tableful of food "—she knows I'm eating like a convict, and is probably wondering whether I can pay for the food. This place *is* just a mile from the prison.''

"Um.'' Brognola picked up his cup. He had ordered no food for himself, only coffee. While he sipped at it, his eyes drifted out the dirty plate-glass window of the restaurant to the busy stretch of state Highway 55 that rolled past them.

Bolan had noticed that something was on Brognola's mind while they were talking at the prison. He was tired of waiting for him to come around to it on his own. "You might as well get it out," he said, after swallowing a mouthful of steak. "You're going to give me indigestion if you keep me in suspense."

Brognola frowned and sat up straight, putting down his coffee. "I need to ask you a favor," he said, avoiding Bolan's eyes.

"Well, I hope it's a simple one." Bolan reached for his own coffee. "You pretty well filled your dance card by asking me to go to prison."

"No more prisons, I promise."

"Let me be more specific," Bolan said. "No more on this Pallonatti thing. I've had it up to—"

"You know how important this is," Brognola interrupted. "This investigation has gone on for years. We're probably just weeks away from handing down major indictments."

"Look, I went into the prison for you and lived side by side with that slimeball for two weeks. You know how I feel about these things."

"Striker, I—"

"Wait a minute." Bolan held up a hand, stopping him. "Let me finish. I've wanted to kill that swaggering bastard every minute of the past two weeks, but I held myself back. I understand that you want to prosecute and need the Giancarlos for your case, but don't ask me to have anything to do with it. Witness protection on this level goes against anything I believe in. Besides, I told you that it was a fluke that Jughead got hit, not a conspiracy."

"We can't afford to take that chance," Brognola replied.

Bolan looked down at his food, his appetite rapidly fading. "You might as well say everything that's on your mind."

The Fed took a breath, reaching out for a quarter of Bolan's club sandwich. "Do you mind?"

Bolan shook his head. "I'm not hungry anymore, anyway."

Brognola bit into the sandwich as if he hadn't eaten for a week. "Let me explain something to you," he said. "This investigation has been going on for more than four years, has run a $35 million tab up on the taxpayer and has tied up literally thousands of manhours. Why? Because we can root them out this time. With the cooperation of the Giancarlos we can dig out the rest of them, wipe out the whole Chicago Mob."

"I have a way of wiping out the Mob, too," Bolan replied. "And it doesn't cost $35 million taxpayer dollars or tie up many manhours. And with my system, they don't come back to cause trouble anymore."

The waitress walked up with dessert, a hot fudge sundae in a tall glass. Bolan put a hand to his stomach and grimaced.

"Put it right here," Brognola said, pushing his coffee cup aside and smiling broadly as the woman set the sundae down. With his fingers he plucked the maraschino cherry from the top of the mound of whipped cream.

"There's more to it than that, Striker," he continued, digging into the sundae with a long spoon. "Your way works great—within limitations—and yes, it's permanent. But it just takes care of the symptoms, not the problem itself. The organization still stands, and it just promotes others to fill the positions you've caused to be vacant. With this investigation we can clean the slate, not just the hoods, but the legitimate businesses they support, the phony charities they run, the pimps they control, the politicians they own...."

"And every time you put one of those animals back on the street under witness protection, *you* are just moving the disease to another part of the country." Bolan sighed, sitting back in the booth. "You can't change these people, Hal. All you're doing is paying a monthly stipend for them to start all over again. I don't know if any amount of testimony is worth that."

"Striker," Brognola said, steam from the fudge rising from his spoon, "by keeping the Giancarlos alive, we can do more good with this one investigation than your guns have ever done. Doesn't that mean something? Besides, I'm not going to ask all that much of you this time."

Bolan looked around the diner to see if they were attracting attention. In the heat of their discussion, their voices had been raised, and it was quiet in the small place in the middle of the afternoon. The pair of truckers drinking coffee at the counter, however, appeared to be caught up in their own road talk.

Bolan meant every word he had said to his friend, but he had to admit that the man had made a few points. "What do you want?" he asked.

"I know how you feel," Brognola answered, "but I don't know where else I can go with this." He put down the spoon beside the half-finished sundae and went back to the club sandwich. "We're ninety percent in agreement with you on the Pallonatti thing. It probably was just a fluke. But that ten percent scares us. We can't afford to let the investigation fall apart this close to the end. Grand Jury hearings, trials, sentencings, backup investigations and indictments are coming real strong right now. We can have this wrapped up in a year or so *if* our witnesses stay cooperative... and alive."

"I think I see what you're getting to," Bolan replied. "If the Pallonatti killing wasn't a fluke—and that's a big *if*—it means witness protection has been cracked. And there's only one way to crack the system—leaks in the department itself."

"Exactly. You operate outside of the departmental structure. No one's likely to know you. You can poke around without rousing a lot of suspicion or departmental paperwork. And I always know, of course, that I can trust you."

"This is a little out of my line, Hal."

"I can give you a few rookie agents," Brognola continued undaunted, "plus Joan Meredith. There're only a handful of people who have any possible access to the witness protection files... a little surveillance might turn up any problems in that area. I'll try and keep you away from the witnesses themselves."

"Could you get me wiretaps?" Bolan asked.

"One way or the other," the man replied.

"Have you thought about relocation?"

"Yeah," the Fed answered. "And we might do it later. But right now nobody wants to relocate if it was a fluke, plus we hate to push the budget for the same reason. Also, if we're leaking on the inside, the relocation would leak, too. You finished?"

"Yeah," Bolan said, and they slid out of the booth. Brognola paid the cashier for the food, getting a receipt for his expense voucher.

As they walked out into the warm October afternoon and climbed into Brognola's rented Ford, Bolan wrestled with his conscience. Despite the big Fed's insistence, he couldn't help but feel that protecting the Giancarlo family for the purpose of hooking bigger fish was a huge mistake. Mafiosi breathed larceny as if it was air and committed murder as casually as most people canceled the newspaper. Yet Brognola had been his best and most dependable friend over the years, and the man's concerns were ones Bolan took seriously. If only it didn't rub so damned hard against the grain.

They took highway 53 and headed north toward the Lewis Lockport Airport, where a Justice Department plane waited to fly them to Washington.

"You know," Brognola remarked after several minutes' silence, "witness protection does a lot more than pay cheap hoods seventeen hundred dollars a month. There are lots of innocent people, victims, we've given a new lease on life to after their testimony. People whose lives wouldn't be worth a nickel otherwise. If there's a hole in the system, they're going to be left without protection, too."

"And by the way, there's another package for you under the front seat."

Bolan leaned down and pulled out a leather bag from under the seat. Inside was the combat harness containing Big Thunder, his .44 AutoMag, and the Beretta 93-R, his surgical instruments for removing the human cancers from the body of mankind. They'd always served as the arbitrator in his disputes with underworld scum, and never once had he had reason to question the finality or justness of their decisions.

"So, what do you think?" Hal asked.

Bolan pulled the Beretta out of its webbing, instinctively checking the load. "I think you've got me against my better judgment," he returned, fixing his friend with hard eyes. "But once I'm in, it's on my terms." He slid the automatic back in its holster. "I make my own decisions."

"I wouldn't want it any other way."

2

Ken Chasen watched the racquet ball bounce just out of his reach, then heard Bert Kaminsky's echoing laughter mixing with the sound of the balls slamming against the wall up and down the court. His timing was just a second off, his reflexes just dulled enough that his entire game was thrown out of sync. He had too much on his mind.

"Whoa!" Kaminsky yelled, running up to slap Chasen on the back. "That's game! I can't believe I finally beat you."

Chasen forced a weak smile. "I guess every dog has his day," he commented as he surveyed the delight on the face of the older, slighter man.

Kaminsky pulled off his soaked sweatband and used it to dry his face. "I prefer to think that my game has finally caught up to yours," he replied, "a fact I shall prove to you the next time we meet." He looked at his watch and made a face. "Oh God, if I'm not out of here in ten minutes I won't live to play again. Let's hit the showers."

Chasen followed him off the brightly lit court, the last in a whole line of courts in the basement of

Justice, and they headed for the locker rooms near the exit. He was nervous now, really nervous, his hand holding the racket in a deathgrip to keep from shaking.

"Any movement on that Teamsters thing?" Kaminsky asked as they entered the white-tiled, brightly lit locker room through the swinging doors.

"We're still taking depositions," Chasen replied. "It's going to be a while yet."

They passed rows of gunmetal-gray lockers, turned down the next-to-last row that was reserved for the Justice Department lawyers and stopped before the doors that had their names taped on the front.

"If we want to docket that case this century," Kaminsky said, "we'll have to build some kind of fire under this thing."

"Hey, boss," Chasen said, sitting on the long bench in front of the lockers, "the whistle blew at five o'clock. Let's save it for the morning."

"You sound like my wife," Kaminsky said, sitting next to Chasen after opening his locker. He struggled out of his knit shirt. "Sure you won't join us tonight for dinner?"

Chasen noticed Kaminsky's clothes hanging in the locker, just like always. He bent down to untie his shoes. "Like to, Bert," he said, "but I promised Marie and the kids I'd take them to a movie. She told me that if she had to listen to one more three-hour Supreme Court discussion, she'd divorce me. I don't think we've done anything that wasn't business related for the past six months."

"I heard that." Kaminsky looked at his watch again, then pulled off his shoes without untying them. He grabbed a towel out of the locker and started toward the showers. "I'd better get a move on," he said.

"Right with you," Chasen said.

Kaminsky moved off, leaving Chasen alone by their lockers. In the silence, distant echoes drifted through the vents, and showers sounded like a spring rain heard through a window.

Chasen sat for a moment, his heart pounding in his chest. It was stupid to be so nervous, he thought. He looked up and down the aisle, then reached a shaking, sweaty hand toward Kaminsky's locker. Everything he had lived by up until that moment was about to go out the window. Every ideal he had ever held was about to be just so much spit in the wind. All for what—a little sex and adventure, a few moments of illicit excitement, a stroking of his middle-aged ego? It didn't make sense no matter how he looked at it, but there he was, shaking like a leaf, getting ready to impugn the security of the country he loved.

The locker pulled wide open, and Chasen quickly got to his feet. Kaminsky's suit hung there neatly. He went for the jacket, his incredibly unresponsive hand reaching for the wallet in the inner pocket. He found it and jerked it out, nearly pulling the suit coat off the hanger.

Calm down...calm down! This wasn't a big deal. Nobody but some scum would get hurt, and then it would all be over. Life would go on, and the whole thing would be forgotten in a week. So why was his heart beating so loudly that he feared Bert could hear it in the shower?

He fumbled open the wallet. Kaminsky was the attorney general's liaison with all the other departments, and was the only man entrusted with the computer codes to all the files in the department.

Chasen opened the flap in the billfold part of the wallet, where he had once seen Kaminsky look to remind himself of a particular computer password. Chasen didn't need access to all the files, of course. There was only one he was interested in.

Two men, talking loudly and laughing, entered the locker room. Chasen froze, unable to move, his fingers stuck in his boss's wallet. The footsteps came closer, the men's conversation centered on Justice Department politics.

His breath caught in his throat, and he closed his eyes tightly, waiting for the inevitable discovery. But the men turned into an aisle several rows before his, and he was temporarily safe.

Chasen took several ragged breaths, then tore back the leather flap. Quickly he pulled out a small, neatly folded piece of paper and he sat down on the bench, putting the wallet beside him. With trembling hands he unfolded the paper.

A long list of names filled the page. A shaking finger slid down the list, stopping abruptly on the words: WITPRO—NEWLIFE. He read the words twice, three times, then hurriedly refolded the paper and put it back in the wallet.

Though witness relocation was Chasen's specialty, the major concern of the department he worked in, he actually knew very little of how the process worked. As a precaution, no one in the department ever actually knew where a witness would be put. The details were all handled on an as-needed basis through channels outside the government, and only the WITPRO file, accessible only at the highest level, provided a list of where witnesses could currently be found.

And now Ken Chasen had joined that select group.

He stood and quickly jammed the wallet back into the suit coat pocket, slamming the door to Kaminsky's locker when he was done. Taking several deep breaths to calm himself, he then stripped off his clothes, grabbed a towel from his own locker and hurried to the showers, meeting Kaminsky on the way out.

"There you are," his boss said as he dried his hair. "If you hurry, I'll walk out to the parking garage with you."

"You'd better go," Chasen replied. His voice sounded odd to him, a trifle hoarse. "I forgot some papers. I'll have to go back up to the office."

"Now who's worrying about work after the five o'clock whistle?" Kaminsky said, his pale eyes dancing playfully.

Chasen desperately searched his reeling brain for a snappy comeback, but couldn't think straight. Instead he merely smiled weakly and entered a shower stall.

The steaming-hot water filled the stall with a vaporous haze, almost an enveloping fog. He soaped himself, but this time the sudsy lather and the gushing water didn't make him feel clean. At any second he expected Kaminsky to come charging back to the showers, demanding to know why Chasen had looked in his wallet.

But it didn't happen.

He stayed in the shower a long time, not wanting to see Kaminsky again today, afraid that his behavior would give something away. He waited for ten, then fifteen minutes, time enough for his boss to have dressed and left three times over. When he finally got out, his body was bright pink from the hot shower.

He dried in the shower room, then walked back to the lockers to dress. No sounds assailed him now. The place was deserted. Even his heart had slowed its pounding.

As he pulled his suit back on, he realized that it could still all end here. If he never used the information he'd acquired, no harm was done. But, as always, the dream broke on the reality of the videotape they had made of him with Yvette, or whatever her name was. He thought about the dissolution of his marriage and the ruin of his career on Capitol Hill, and realized that if he didn't take the next step, he'd merely be another body thrown on the scrap heap, another promising career shot dead before its prime.

Someone had once told him that he'd rather be a has-been than a never-was. Now, as he shoehorned into his loafers, those words came back to him. Sure, he'd use the password he'd stolen. At this point he'd do anything to save his image. He hadn't worked his whole life and graduated eighth in his class at Harvard and eaten governmental shit for the past ten years just to throw it all away over the lives of a few cheap hoods. There was nothing wrong in what he was doing. Anybody would do the same thing in his shoes.

Wouldn't they?

He swung the locker closed, its sound reverberating through the entire basement like a solitary outcry. He walked out of the locker, past the Marine corporal at the checkpoint, and back into the building proper, taking the elevator up to the offices on the fourth floor.

The main door of his suite of offices was marked: Witness Protection and Relocation. It was locked, testifying to the staff's quick weekend getaway. He used his key, moving into the darkened suite.

Instead of going to his own office and the computer terminal in there, he opted instead for that of his colleague, Chuck Davis. Somehow he'd feel better running this through someone else's machinery.

After using the phone to dial himself into the main trunk feed, he quickly called up the witness protection file, using his newly acquired password, NEW-LIFE, to force the secrets of the files out into the open. When the password actually got him into the secret file, he was surprised to feel a pang of regret. He realized that he'd been hoping the attempt would fail, but that success was being forced upon him.

The computer prompted him for names, its cursor flashing impatiently. With shaking fingers he tapped out four names on the keyboard: Perezzi, V.; Ottoni, M.; Barberi, F.; Giancarlo, S. Quickly and without conscience, the machine coughed up four aliases and addresses, in four widely separated states.

He copied them down on a scratch pad, tore off the sheet and folded it and put it in his shoe. He picked up the phone on Chuck's desk and dialed from memory the number of the Econolodge on the outskirts of the city—a place he had gotten to know well over the course of the past two months.

"Econolodge, Washington," came the voice.

"Five-eighteen, please," Chasen said, the number ringing almost before he finished saying it.

Yvette answered on the third ring. "Darling, is that you?"

"I've got it," he said simply. "I'm on my way."

"Good luck, my—"

He hung up on her, then immediately wanted to re-dial and apologize, but forced himself not to. No matter how badly he tried to think of the woman, he had a difficult time blaming her for the things that had happened.

Ultimately he could only blame himself.

Feeling a guilty sense of excitement, he dialed home and told his wife that he'd be working late again tonight.

SECURITY-LOCKED DOORS were the specialty of the Econolodge. Security-locked doors and the indoor swimming pool. Beyond that, the motel was a cheap place in a bad end of a bad town. Just the kind of place to be chosen for romantic trysts because the guilty lovers figured no one they knew would use it. So much for originality.

Chasen walked down the hallway toward 518, feeling betrayed, disgusted and excited all at the same time. Yvette was the most incredible woman he'd ever known. She loved with total abandon, giving everything of herself to him as if he were the only man on earth. After eight years of marriage and two kids, Marie's brand of companionship and quiet love couldn't hold a candle to one hour with Yvette. It scared him to think that he quite possibly was capable of selling out his country to her even if the videotape didn't exist.

He reached the door to room 518 and hesitated before knocking. This was it, though. Too much had gone past for them to carry on as before. He'd deliver the information, pick up his tape and walk out for good and all. This time, he resolved, he would break the string.

When she opened the door, her eyes were moist, slightly red from crying. Her blond hair was loose, gently caressing her shoulders. "Oh, Ken..." she said breathlessly, throwing open the door and drawing him inside.

Before he knew what was happening she was in his arms, her body warm and yielding as she clung to him for dear life. "My darling," she cried into his shoulder. "I'm so sorry for all this. I feel so cheap...so dirty, I..."

"Shh," he whispered, lost in the fragrance of her hair, the way her pelvis undulated gently against him, arousing him despite his intention of walking right out. "It's not your fault, baby."

She loosened her embrace and held him at arm's length, looking into his eyes, her body lush under the low-cut, knit dress she wore. "Do you really mean that? Oh darling, it was so awful. They forced me to put that camera in here, I...wish..."

"Why?" he asked, following her from the small entry into the bedroom.

She sat down on the bed, kicking off her shoes. "My...brother had been in trouble and needed legal help. I borrowed a lot of money that I couldn't p-pay back."

Yvette began crying softly. Chasen sat next to her on the bed and put an arm protectively around her. "They gave me three options," she sobbed, laying her head on his chest. "I could either d-die, or become their prostitute, or...meet you."

"Me specifically?" Chasen asked, slowly falling backward and taking her with him so they were both prone on the bed.

She shook her head and rolled over to cuddle with him. "One night another girl took me to Phillips restaurant and pointed out you and some others as Justice Department lawyers in the bar there."

"You and I met at Phillips," Chasen said, and kissed her tenderly on the lips, her mouth softening under his.

"Yes," she said. "I came back several times until I was able to get you alone."

"Why me?"

"I liked you," she said. "You seemed nice...gentle. I swear I didn't know what they wanted me to do. All I knew was that they promised to forget my debt if I did them this favor and got to know you. I guess then I f-fell in love."

Her hand was resting on his hip, massaging softly, exciting him. While he was still able to think, he sat up and took off his shoe, pulling out the piece of paper.

"Here it is," he said. "Will this end it?"

"I hope it doesn't end us." She took the paper from him. "Unzip me, will you?"

He pulled down the zipper tab on the back of her dress, his hands shaking from excitement. When she stood and let the dress slide to the floor, he discovered she wore nothing under it, her body more beautiful than he remembered.

Yvette stepped out of the dress and picked up a videotape from the top of the television set. "Here's the tape," she said, tossing it on the bed. "It's yours. It's all over now."

From her purse on the dresser she extracted a plastic bag full of white powder. "They also said to give you this, to show there are no hard feelings."

Chasen took the bag from her, staring at evidence of the other vice he had picked up since he met Yvette. There was a lot more cocaine there than he had ever imagined existed, at least several ounces. Had he not already sold his soul, he would have given back the drug. But in for a penny, he figured, in for a pound.

"Why don't you get undressed," she said, the tip of her tongue moistening her already inviting lips, "while I make sure the door is locked."

He nodded. His fingers were already unbuttoning his shirt as Yvette walked out of his sight, through the entry hall to the door, the paper locked firmly in her grasp.

Quietly she opened the door. A man stood just outside. When he saw that she was naked, he grinned.

Without a word, she handed him the piece of paper, winking as she closed and locked the door.

3

The image was fuzzy—bright white, dull pink interspersed with splotches of reds and yellows. Burnett grunted and pulled away, using the small sewing machine screwdriver to adjust the Bushnell scope's focus. He moved up to the eyepiece and fine-tuned with the screwdriver.

The image sharpened, the cross hairs pulling into fine black lines in the center of the focus. He could see her now, his mystery woman, in the bathroom on the third floor of the apartment building that served as off-campus housing for J.C. Smith University, across Freedom Drive from his boardinghouse. Burnett didn't know her name and didn't care. All that mattered to him was that he held her life in his hands on a daily basis. Any time he wanted to, he could snuff her out, penetrate her, possess her in ways that other men never could. The power of it excited him, and he wiped at a line of sweat on his upper lip with the back of his hand, which wore a leather glove with the fingers cut out.

She stood naked in front of the mirror, steam from the shower drifting from behind the plastic curtain.

Her jet-black hair spilled out of her hands as she piled it atop her head to fit beneath the shower cap with daisies printed on it. The cross hairs of the rifle rested about the middle of her arm. Leaning back, he cranked up the tripod just a notch, bringing the sights up to the middle of her head.

"Yeah," he whispered, his breathing shallow.

He took a step back from the sights, enjoying the feel of his superior position, enjoying the darkness of his room. The Brown Precision rifle that the scope was attached to was silhouetted on its tripod against the dim light that entered his room from the outside. He ran his hand softly, lightly along the length of the fiberglass stock, pausing for a second at the bolt before pulling it back hard.

He leaned down to the sights again. The woman entered the shower, her form just a bare outline against the pale-pink shower curtain. He cranked up the sighting just a touch, again going for the hint of a head, as if she were a deer hiding in the brush.

She was his now, all his, not like other women, pushy women who expected too much from a man, women who wanted to control men without respect for the natural dominance of the male. No, his mystery lady was his alone to do with as he chose—her life or death all in his power.

A single bullet lay on the table next to the tripod. Burnett scooped it up and squeezed it in his hand. A 458 Magnum, it was big, big enough to rip away half the mystery lady's head and still bury itself deeply in the wall behind. He could do it to her, do it right now if he wanted.

His lips were dry. He licked them, then leaned forward to drop the cartridge into the open chamber. It went in clean, snug. He leaned down to the scope again, his fingers idly toying with the bolt. She was still in the shower, still in his sights, and the desire was nearly overpowering.

He grabbed the bolt hard, shoving the bullet into the guts of the rifle. She was now a finger twitch away from the experience of her lifetime. He laughed low. He was in control, his finger tracing and retracing the trigger guard as he watched her open the shower curtain and step out of the tub.

His finger ached for the trigger, longing to share its power with the object of his affections. He touched it, backing off only slightly. How far could he pull it without actually firing the gun?

The phone rang loudly. It jerked him away from the weapon, dropping him heavily from the emotional peak he had climbed.

"Shit," he spit, groping his way through the dark room until he found the phone under a pile of dirty fatigues. This had better be good. He ripped the receiver off its cradle and brought it to his mouth.

"Burnett," he said.

"Mr. Burnett," came a soft-spoken voice, one he recognized from previous conversations. "This is Jericho."

Burnett turned and took a furtive look through his window. Hundreds of feet distant, his mystery lady's light was just one of many. "Yeah," he said, running a gloved hand across his severe crewcut. "I was beginning to think I wouldn't hear from you no more."

"You're hearing from me now," Jericho responded, "and I have the job I promised you."

"Sure," Burnett said. He was skeptical. Nearly forty people had responded to his ad in *Soldier of Fortune* magazine, but they'd either been reporters looking for an easy story, or people who wanted their spouses knocked off for a share of the insurance money. "I want you to know that I'm going to have to have enough bucks up front to finance my end of things."

"Would a half million in unmarked cash help in that regard?" Jericho asked.

Burnett forced his voice to professional calm. "That should be sufficient," he said, then struck out blind. "With another half million due on completion of the mission."

Jericho's voice came through with a chilling undercurrent of humor. "Done," the man said. "Now listen carefully, here are your instructions. Go to the Greyhound bus depot in downtown Charlotte. In the men's room, in the third stall from the left, you will find a key taped to the back of the commode. That key will open a locker there in the terminal. In the locker will be a small valise, containing your down payment plus a list of targets. The more quickly you dispose of the targets, the better your chances of living to spend all that money—understood?"

"Yeah," Burnett said. "But how do I get back to you to collect the rest of the cash when I'm done?"

"We'll just have to trust each other, Mr. Burnett. How do I know that you won't simply take my half million and leave the country?"

It was Burnett's turn to laugh. "If you knew me, Jericho, you'd know that I'd probably do this for nothing. I'm a man who loves his work."

"I'll take you at your word," Jericho replied. "Please take me at mine. When you conclude our business, I'll be in touch, with the rest of the cash. It's not a bad deal considering the fact that I'm overpaying you fourfold in just the first installment. If you never heard from me again, you'd still come out way ahead."

"Right," Burnett said, finally getting on even footing. "And if I didn't come through, you'd probably hire someone else and pay them more to come and kill *me*."

"You're very perceptive. I think we'll enjoy a satisfactory association."

"Third stall from the left," Burnett repeated, trying to implant the instructions firmly in his mind.

"Would you like to write it down?"

"Yeah...sure." Burnett looked around the darkened room, having no idea where to find anything to write with. Third from the left. "Got it."

"You're on your own at this point," Jericho said. "Don't wait too long to get started."

Jericho hung up then, leaving Burnett to stare at the receiver in his hand. There'd be little chance of his waiting long to get started. This was the life he had chosen for himself and now someone had dropped enough cash on him to make the dream come true. Goodbye post office pay.

Suddenly he realized the phone was buzzing dial tone, and he hung it up and moved back to the rifle, to peer intently through the scope. She was gone, and the bathroom was dark. He pulled back the bolt, the cartridge popping out into his hand. Soon, very soon, it wouldn't be a game anymore.

He could hardly wait.

MACK BOLAN PULLED the plastic top off the Styrofoam cup and brought the steaming coffee to his lips. It tasted bitter, metallic.

Brognola had gotten him this apartment on New York Avenue, barely a mile from the White House, furnished with a generous allotment of electronic equipment undoubtedly appropriated from GAO warehouses. Wiretap confirmation still wasn't forthcoming, but Brognola had told Bolan not to let his agents worry about that temporary omission. That statement meant, "You're on your own, Lone Ranger. Don't get caught."

"We've got it set, Mr. Belasko," came the voice of Benny Young from the bedroom.

"Right there," Bolan called. He walked through the spacious living room, where several lamps stood on the polished wood floors, and walked into the bedroom. Four people occupied the room, their sleeping bags and personal articles filling the floor space. They were young, younger than he remembered ever being, and were eager to succeed on their first real assignment as Justice Department investigators. Bolan didn't want to be the one to tell them that nothing from this mission would go into the active files, and that the satisfaction of doing the right thing was the only reward they'd take away from this assignment.

Benny Young sat on a folding chair in front of a large electronics board, switching toggles on and off as he ran a troubleshooting check. Standing beside him was a woman named Carol Niven. She studied the board carefully, trying to commit it to memory. Sitting cross-legged on the floor playing gin were Roy Carver, a black man who wore a permanent scowl, and redheaded Neal Lomax, both hardcases who had washed out at the CIA farm in Pennsylvania and taken a transfer to Justice. Brognola had said they were too "political" to work for the Company, which, translated, meant that they questioned orders on ideological principles, not a good trait in a job that required shifting allegiances on an almost daily basis. None of that bothered Bolan as long as they did the right thing under pressure.

"Are we on stream?" he asked Benny as he picked his way around sleeping bags and portable radios to get to the board.

"Yes, sir," Benny replied, flipping a last toggle that made the whole board light up. "We've got all ten houses wired through here. The lines are voice-activated so they'll record only the conversations as they are placed, and shut themselves down with silence."

"What if there's more than one phone call at a time?" Bolan asked.

The woman answered. "This will record up to five conversations simultaneously, each one going onto a separate cassette."

"And if you want to monitor," Young went on, "the turn of a dial will give you live sound right here."

"Good." Bolan was satisfied with the arrangements so far. "This will get us started."

"Started doing what?" Carver asked.

"That's a good question." Bolan pulled up a folding chair and sat down. He tried another sip of coffee and grimaced as he put it down. "I'm not going to lie to you and build this up into a big thing, because it probably isn't. As Hal told you, we're doing a little interdepartmental surveillance to make sure there are no leaks in witness protection. What it amounts to, basically, is taking shifts here at the board and some shadowboxing with people who aren't conforming to their routines."

"What are we looking for, exactly?" Lomax asked, putting down his cards and turning to face Bolan.

"Contacts," Bolan replied. "Anything out of the ordinary. If addresses are being leaked, they're being leaked *to* somebody. Hopefully, if a leak is there, the wiretaps will pick it up or a stakeout might turn up something. It's a long shot, but one that won't waste a great deal of time. If there's a leak where we're most concerned, something's probably going to happen soon."

"It seems to me," Young commented thoughtfully, "that the damage may already have been done."

"I told you it was a long shot," Bolan replied. "Though it's possible that leaks of this nature could perhaps be ongoing."

"Am I late?" came a voice from the door. Bolan looked up to see Joan Meredith standing in the doorway with an armload of takeout food in white paper bags. "Nobody ever thinks of bringing food to these things."

"All right!" Carver said with enthusiasm. "The brains of the outfit just showed up."

"It's just hamburgers and fries," Joan explained as she passed a bag to Carver.

Lomax grinned. "Sounds like heaven to me." He reached into one of the bags.

"The last time I saw you," Bolan told Joan, remembering a firefight in San Francisco, "you had a cast on your arm."

"And the last time I saw you, you said you'd stay in touch."

Bolan shrugged. "So...we're in touch," he replied. "Everyone, this is Joan Meredith...an associate."

There were introductions all around, and Joan settled into the discussion. Bolan was glad to see her. She looked good, a little sadder and wiser, but it agreed with her.

"Officially," Bolan said once they got started again, "we don't exist, nor does this investigation."

"Then who the hell sanctioned it?" Carver asked, frowning.

"I don't know," Bolan replied. "But I trust Hal Brognola, and I'm going to ask you to trust me. What we have here are ten names, from the attorney general down through the secretaries who work in witness protection and relocation. All of these people have worked with the computer programs where the information is held, all of them possibly have, or have had, access to this classified information."

"I'm assuming you're joking," Carol Niven said, "when you say the attorney general is suspect."

Bolan looked her dead in the eye. "I don't joke," he said. "The attorney general is line two. And I mean what I say," Bolan said harshly, ready to take the edge of fun off the proceedings. "I'm telling you this, if there is or has been a real leak, the person or people responsible will do anything to keep their identity a secret. We'll keep this flexible; we'll keep it liquid—but if it turns serious, be prepared for anything."

He pulled a small stack of index cards out of his pocket, handing some to each of the others and keeping several for himself. "Tonight, we'll spend a little time at one of the suspects' residences, trying to get a feel for their habits, bedtimes, etcetera. Benny, you'll take the first watch on the board. Tomorrow we'll get to work on their morning and lunch routines. Fortunately they all work at the same place, so that should make things somewhat easier. Keep it loose. Follow your instincts.''

"What if we get caught?'' Niven said.

"You have no official standing, and none of the rest of us has ever seen you before. So *don't* get caught.''

"THIS IS BULLSHIT, Burnett,'' Rex Jasper said as he followed the man down the long, tiled hallway that led to the men's room in the bus station basement. "Ain't nobody gonna leave a bunch of money laying around a bus station.''

"You'll see bullshit in about five minutes,'' Burnett replied, pushing through the doorway and into the vacant, brightly lit john. "Coolie, take the door.''

"Coolie'' Powell, so named because of the long queue in which he wore his dark hair, stationed himself by the bathroom door while Burnett and Jasper approached the five stalls opposite a small bank of sinks. Powell and Burnett were both wearing the fatigue shirts they had worn in Vietnam, with the sleeves and airborne patches cut off. Jasper wore his traditional Hawaiian shirt with a cowboy hat, a large buck knife hanging from his belt.

Burnett stopped at the third cubicle from the left. He'd had nothing but a steady stream of disbelief from Jasper ever since they'd gotten in the car to come down here, and he'd had about enough. He tried to open the door of the stall and found that it was locked.

"What the hell . . .''

"It's a pay toilet." Jasper laughed. "You're not only gonna get screwed, you're gonna hafta *pay* for it!"

"Shut up and give me a quarter."

"If I had a quarter," Jasper said, "you think I'd be following you around like Mary's little lamb?"

Burnett scowled at him, then raised a jungle-booted foot, smashing the door open and knocking it right off the hinges.

"Damn!" Jasper said. "Don't make so much noise. I gotta pocketful of nose candy on me. If the cops..."

Burnett swung around to him, grabbing the front of Jasper's shirt and twisting hard. "What the hell are you doing bring dope into a situation like this?" he demanded in a harsh whisper. "I oughta cut your throat right here, you son of a bitch."

"Burnett, I—"

"Someone's coming," Coolie said from the doorway.

Burnett pushed Jasper away from him. "Take a whiz," he ordered.

Jasper moved to stand in front of one of the urinals while Burnett went into the third stall and stood by the door, holding it on its hinges. Coolie lit a cigarette and leaned against the wall. Within seconds a middle-aged Japanese man walked into the room, a small suitcase in his hand.

He stopped dead upon seeing the thugs. "Please to excuse," he said, and turned around, leaving quickly.

Burnett let the door go and turned to the commode to feel around behind the cold porcelain. He found the key at once and ripped it off the toilet. Shoving aside the broken door, he stepped out of the stall and held up the key in front of Jasper's face.

"Tell me about bullshit now," he said, eyes narrowing.

"I didn't think..." Jasper replied, letting the unfinished sentence serve as his acknowledgment that Burnett was right and he was wrong.

"C'mon, let's try this baby," Coolie said, stepping up to stare in fascination at the key, and by so doing, dissipating the tension. Burnett shrugged and decided to say no more to Jasper.

They left the men's room and took the hallway back to the stairs, then climbed up to the main floor of the terminal. It was late on a Friday night, no one around but scabs, bums and the homeless, looking for a place to sleep. The bus stations of America had become the last dumping ground of the chronic indigent, those without transportation in a society built around transportation. An air of hopelessness hung over everyone there. Burnett hated the sight of them. They reminded him too much of his own upbringing. A beat cop stood leaning against the ticket counter, chewing tobacco and keeping an eye on things. And right now his eye was on Burnett.

Burnett returned the cop's stare boldly then moved past him to the bank of lockers by the west door of the terminal. Jasper and Coolie gathered around him as he turned the key in the bright orange locker whose number, 23, matched that of the key.

It opened easily. Inside was a large satchel, just as Jericho had said. Burnett pulled the bag out of the locker and shut the door. He wiped his nose on his half-gloved hand and smiled. "In this bag is our future, my friends."

"Yeah," Coolie agreed, eyes bright. "Let's open it."

"Outside." Burnett nodded toward the cop. "In the car."

The three exited the terminal into the rapidly cooling evening, the smell of diesel fumes heavy in the air. They crossed the parking lot and headed down Tryon Street, where the Wacovia Bank tower and the gold dome of the civic center dominated the drab downtown landscape. The bag was heavy, Burnett noticed. There was something inside it.

His '71 Chevy was parked half a block from the terminal, away from streetlights where a police cruiser might see that the license plate was two years out of date.

They climbed into the old, gray vehicle, Jasper up front with Burnett, and Coolie in the back. He leaned over the seat to watch the opening of the bag.

"This is really weird," he said. "I mean, what do you really know about this Jericho character. I—"

"You talk too much," Burnett interrupted as he thumbed the catch release on the satchel. The lid popped up. He opened the car door a crack, so the dome light would help them examine the contents.

"Oh sweet baby!" Coolie's eyes widened when he saw the bundles of cash. "I can hardly believe it!"

"Jesus!" Burnett said, pulling out several bundles. "This is the real thing."

"Whoo!" Coolie yelled, and began laughing wildly. "This is incredible!"

A manila envelope lay in the bag amid the stacks of money. Burnett pulled it out and opened it. Several photographs fell out, each one with a name, address and alias clipped to it. "Well boys," he said, "now we got to earn all this bread." He looked at the addresses. "Think we'll start in sunny Southern California tomorrow night. What do you say?"

"All right...L.A.!" Coolie yelped, waving a stack of twenties in front of his face.

Burnett smiled, then turned to Jasper, who was staring in disbelief at the money. Jasper looked up and met his eyes. He shook his head. "Count me out, man," he said. "This has all been a kick...but, God, now we got to go out and kill people."

"We've all killed before," Burnett said.

"That was in war, man," Jasper said. "Hell, I'd go into the jungle with you and shoot some dinks, but this...this I can't do."

Burnett smiled. His hand slid slowly down his leg to his left boot and found the handle of the Ka-bar knife he always kept there. "You should've thought of all that before, *compadre*."

"I never thought anybody would really answer that stupid ad. It was just a game, you know?"

"No, I don't know," Burnett replied. He whipped the Ka-bar out of his boot and jammed it straight into Jasper's throat.

The man's eyes went wide and he tried to say something, but a rush of blood came out instead of words. Burnett pulled out the knife. Jasper's hands went to his throat in disbelief, his lips still moving silently as the severed jugular poured thick liquid down his front.

"You're yellow, Jasper," Burnett said casually, while reaching across the dying man to open the car door. "And there's nothing I hate worse than a coward."

He shoved hard, and the already weakened Jasper tumbled out of the car and onto the street. Coolie quickly climbed over the seat and took Jasper's place, closing the door as Burnett started the engine and pulled away from the curb.

"I know where we can get a few more guys," Burnett said. "But let's not tell them how much dough we've got, okay?"

"Fine by me." Coolie juggled two stacks of bills. "That's just fine by me."

Burnett drove down Tryon, looking once in the rearview mirror. Jasper had struggled to his feet, and was staggering toward the bus station. He took three steps before his knees gave out and he fell hard to the street, dying as his blood ebbed away into the gutter.

4

Bolan and Joan Meredith sat in the rented Chevy in the small, private parking garage in D.C. and watched the seafood restaurant with the big lobster on the sign across the street. Carol Niven and Roy Carver sat in their separate cars elsewhere in the lot, also watching the restaurant.

"I wish we were on the inside and they were on the outside," the woman said, leaning her head back on the seat. "This damned surveillance is for the birds."

Bolan grunted. Patience was a virtue he had learned long ago. He looked at his watch. "If it goes anything like last night they shouldn't be in there too much longer."

"Do they always come here after work?" Meredith asked.

"It's a favorite hangout of people in the department," Bolan replied, watching the dying sun as it glinted in orange-pink sabers on the gently rippling Potomac, the Capitol buildings just distant silhouettes against the rapidly darkening sky. "They stop in the bar for a few drinks, then head for home about seven-thirty. I've heard it called an attitude adjustment hour.'' Bolan's ironic tone told what he thought of that expression.

"That's where I wish I was," she said, "home, soaking myself and my arm in a nice hot bath."

"The arm still give you trouble?" he asked.

"It stiffens up sometimes, especially in cold weather." She looked at him quizzically. "How about you, Mack? Where's home for you?"

He half smiled at her. "Right now it's this car, I suppose. I'm always on the move...so I really don't have a permanent base of operation."

She shook her head. "You know, it's really sad to hear you call home a base of operation."

He didn't answer right away, then just said, "By the way, make sure you don't call me Mack in front of the others."

"Don't worry, Mr. Belasko, your secret is safe with me." She stared through the windshield. "Look, here comes one of them."

Bolan watched one of the witness protection lawyers come out of the restaurant. It was a man in his early fifties, wearing a black suit—Bert Kaminsky, Carver's man for the night. Bolan hit the horn a light tap, Carver responding in kind and starting his engine several cars farther down the line.

Kaminsky's white Porsche came humming out of the restaurant lot and passed beneath their vantage point, Carver following seconds later.

"For my money," Meredith said, "he's our main suspect. He's got direct access, plus he likes a fancy life-style."

"You might study him a little more," Bolan replied. "He was born wealthy, so the life-style is actually one he's always known and taken for granted. Plus, he helped head up the New York State Crime Commission back in the fifties that led to the Congressional hearings—"

"That broke the back of the Mob in New York," Meredith finished. "You're right. I should do my homework better."

"I'm not counting him out," Bolan conceded, "but he's at the bottom of my list. He seems like a good, honest man."

"Here comes another one," she said, referring to her photo book of suspects. "It's . . . Ken Chasen."

"He's mine." Bolan started the engine.

The woman pushed open her door. "I'd better get back to my own car. It looks like they're all leaving."

"Remember," he said, "anything unusual . . . report in to Benny Young back at base."

"Base," she repeated, once again looking sadly at Bolan.

"Later," he said as she closed the door. He backed out of his space and drove to the pay window, the gate going up to allow him out just as Chasen's Corvette passed him.

He pulled up easily behind the Corvette when it stopped at a red light half a block farther on. Bolan was about to put on his left blinker, prepared to follow the man home, but instead Chasen turned right and headed away from town.

Bolan followed at a respectable distance, the Vette easy enough to keep in sight. In about ten minutes, Chasen guided his car into the covered parking of the Econolodge motel.

Strange, Bolan thought, gliding into the front parking lot near the office. He turned out his headlights and watched. A moment later Chasen came out of the garage, looked all around and entered the building. Bolan got out of the Chevy and followed him in.

Chasen had just disappeared behind the closing doors of an elevator as Bolan crossed the lobby. The big man turned back toward the registration desk, passing a glassed-in pool that smelled strongly of chlorine.

"You got a Ken Chasen registered here?" he asked the man working the night desk.

The guy went through his reservation listings, frowning. "No," he said, looking up.

"Thanks." Bolan headed for a pay phone near the front door and dialed up the apartment HQ.

"Yeah?" Young answered on the first ring.

"Belasko," Bolan said. "I'm at the Econolodge Inn on the eastern edge of the city. My man, Chasen, ended up here instead of going home. Maybe it's legit...maybe he's just meeting his secretary or something on business. I'll stay on it here until he goes."

"Got it," Young said. "Good luck."

"Thanks." Bolan hung up the phone, though he at this point figured he needed coffee more than luck.

UNTIL HE HAD SOME, Burnett didn't know how little money meant to him and how easy it was to spend. The big white Cadillac had cost a bundle, but so what? It felt good to be on top of the world for a change. Why worry about holding on to a buck when a guy could snuff out at any time? Enjoy, that was Burnett's motto. If anyone thought that a bit simplistic, they'd just have to lump it—just like those clowns down on the beach.

He watched them through binoculars from his car, parked on the shoulder of California 1, the coastal highway. The Pacific Ocean washed noisily up on Laguna Beach below their redwood deck. They laughed, drank wine and talked about things he'd probably never know or understand. He hated them for owning a beach house, while wanting one for himself. He hated the men for the women they attracted so casually. He hated the women for being so accessible to that kind of man. Most of all he hated the men and women both because they stood in the way of his enjoying himself with the rest of his money. When they died, when the others died, he could then take their place on the social ladder and enjoy his money to the full.

Besides, he liked watching things die, a fact he had known from childhood and that had been confirmed in Vietnam. He loved the power, the control. He loved to kill people up close so he could watch their eyes as the light drained out and he could stand above them to assert his superiority.

"When we gonna do it?" asked the big man who sat next to him.

"Soon, Juke." Burnett turned to stare at the large, retarded man with the oversize head, who had walked out of a mental institution and into Burnett's life a couple of months before. "We've got to let the sun get down a little more first."

Burnett seemed to have a knack for attracting a certain type of person, what most people would think of as turning up bad pennies. Burnett tended to think of it as extremely good luck.

He stared out at the ocean, at the sun disappearing on its distant horizon. He didn't notice the beauty of the sunset, the many shades of pink streaking the sky in pastel splendor, nor did he react to the inscrutable majesty of the rolling, blue-gray waters. All he saw was ten more minutes of daylight, ten more minutes separating him from his mission.

The walkie-talkie beside him on the leather seat squawked to life. "Blue Team leader, this is Red Team leader... over."

Burnett picked up the unit and pushed the button on the side. "This is Blue Team leader... what's up, Coolie? Over."

"We are in position in front of the house," came Coolie's staticky voice. "The front door is locked, but we can go right through the picture window. Over."

"Hold your position, Red Team," Burnett said. "We are preparing to flank them. Over."

"Cleavon says we should get on with it. Over."

Burnett's jaw tightened. He hadn't wanted Cleavon on this mission, which was why he had originally chosen Jasper. The man was dangerous enough, all right, but his militant hatred of most whites made him tend to lose control too often.

"You tell Cleavon that *I* am in charge of this operation, and if he doesn't like it he can walk right now. We don't need him. Over."

"Roger. Out."

The big man beside him chuckled. "Cleavon's mad," he said, then did an imitation of Cleavon's face when he was angry, which made him laugh again.

Burnett drew a long breath, then exhaled. There was one bright spot about using Juke and Cleavon. He had given each of them five grand for the operation instead of the hundred thousand Jasper would have collected, and they were as happy as pigs in slop. Juke probably would have done it for slop. He followed Burnett around like a puppy dog, blindly doing anything the man asked of him.

He looked at his watch, but had to turn on the map light to see it. It was nearly dark enough. Picking up the binoculars he spied on the dinner party again. Two men and two women were sitting out on the high deck. The men were leaning back in their chairs smoking, while the women sat engaged in their inane woman chatter. Even as he watched, though, one of the men extinguished his cigar and one of the women gathered up the drained coffee cups and put them on a tray. The party would soon be breaking up.

It was time to move. Burnett focused on the man in the white shirt and pants, then looked again at the photo on the seat of the car. It was a positive make, no sweat.

"C'mon," he said. "Let's get down there."

He opened his door and stepped out onto the roadway, bringing the walkie-talkie. The ocean lay about a hundred feet below, down a long rolling hillside. They had parked just around a curve in the road, just far enough off the road that no one could see the car until they were passing it. It seemed safe enough to leave it there. This would only take a couple of minutes.

He put the key in the trunk lock, and like everything else on the expensive car, it seemed to open automatically, the lid rising slowly.

He pulled out the pale green duffel bag with U.S. Marine Corps stenciled on it and handed it to Juke. "Keep the gear from rattling," he said, "and as we maneuver the hill, try and keep low, beneath the underbrush."

Juke smiled stupidly. "Okay, Burnett," he said in a loud voice.

"And no talking," Burnett said. "Just keep your mouth shut."

Juke started to respond, then stopped himself, grinning instead and pointing to his mouth to indicate his lips were sealed.

Burnett hoisted a leg over the retaining wire on the edge of the shoulder and started down the hill, his fatigue clothing blending with the scrub oak and the shadows of descending night. Behind him, he could hear Juke puffing, out of shape, but keeping up despite the heavy ordnance he was carrying.

They reached the beach within two minutes, coming out of the brush thirty feet from the deck where the dinner party was winding down. The sun had set now, the tall pylons that supported the deck a dark forest of shadows. Crouching, Burnett turned to Juke, who was sitting on the ground, breathing heavily. He pointed to the underside of the deck. Juke swallowed hard and nodded.

Still in a crouch, Burnett charged across the open sand to the safety of the deck supports. When he reached the shadows, he motioned for Juke to follow, and the big man lumbered over.

Burnett leaned against one of the pylons, an old telephone pole, and looked straight up into the darkness of the underside of the deck. The faint sounds of conversation and laughter drifted down to him. Nothing suspicious. He turned oceanward. A long flight of wooden steps led down from the deck to the beach, the ocean itself fifty feet distant. He felt the same surge of excitement that search-and-destroy missions in Vietnam had always aroused in him.

He turned down the sound of the walkie-talkie and brought it to his lips, pressing the button. "This is Blue Team leader to Red Team leader...over."

"Yeah...let's go," came Cleavon's voice through the small speaker.

"Where the hell's Coolie?" Burnett asked in a harsh whisper, then added as an afterthought, "Over."

"Just tell me what you want," Cleavon demanded harshly. "I'm gettin' old standin' out here with my dick in my hand."

The rage was creeping up on Burnett, but he fought it back as best he could. "We go in one minute," he said, voice trembling. "Are you looking at your watch? Over."

"You said one minute," Cleavon returned. "I know how long a minute is. Just do it, soldier boy."

"You'd better be there, asshole," Burnett threatened. "And listen to me . . . nobody gets out of there alive except us. Okay . . . a minute from . . . now. Out."

He reached out and took the duffel from Juke and unzipped it, pulling out two Remington 12-gauge pump shotguns and two .45 automatics. "You hear what I told Cleavon?" he whispered to Juke as they both stuck the .45s into the waistbands of their pants. "Kill everyone, Juke. We have to kill everyone."

The big man nodded, still keeping his promise of silence, his eyes wide.

Burnett pumped a round into the chamber, feeling powerful and manly. He nodded to Juke there in the darkness, then charged across the sand to the stairs, running up them two at a time.

The diners saw him as soon as he crested the deck. One of the women screamed as his pigeon jumped to his feet, the cigar falling out of his mouth. The man was turning toward the house as the sound of the front picture window imploding heralded the arrival of Red Team.

Burnett took in details about the four with a sweeping glance. The two women wore designer clothes; the pigeon, as host, was dressed more casually than the other man, who wore a suit and looked wimpy and confused. The man in white put his hands up, just as Coolie and Cleavon came through the sliding-glass door to the patio.

The man in white tightened his jaw angrily. Burnett was surprised to see he wasn't scared. "You're from Villani, right?" he said. "I can pay you better...I swear I can."

The man could have offered the moon right then and it wouldn't have mattered to Burnett. He was so keyed up with the urge to kill that he would have exploded if he couldn't have found release. His breath was coming too fast for him to talk, his lips stretched across his teeth in a tight grin.

He raised the shotgun, grunting, beyond words, and caressed the trigger for only a second before squeezing it. The obscene pop of the weapon triggered more screams from the women as the man's chest exploded all over his white shirt and he fell to his knees. Coolie fired then from behind, taking off the top of the man's head and throwing him forward on the deck, dead on impact.

Juke and the laughing Cleavon Brown cut loose on the other man as he tried to dive over the edge of the deck. Scattershot knocked him sideways and he took out the rail as his body plummeted to the sand below. Both Coolie and Burnett turned to the woman still sitting, stupefied, at the table and opened up on her at the same time. The glass of the tabletop and wine bottles exploded as her head and torso were ripped apart. Cleavon fired at her, too, knocking her out of the chair to the deck.

The lone survivor stood, hands to her face, screaming insanely amid the carnage.

"Mine!" Burnett yelled before the others could do her.

He threw down the shotgun and drew the .45, walking to her and grabbing her by her long, blond hair, jerking her head back. He looked deeply into her panic-stricken eyes, wanting her to take the image of his superiority with her to the beyond. Her scream caught in her throat, her mouth hanging open.

He jammed the semiautomatic into her stomach and pulled the trigger, the sound muffled somewhat by her body. She began shaking wildly. He fired again, clamping his mouth on hers for a long, lingering kiss of death.

She slid to the deck. Burnett looked up with glazed eyes, his face and mouth covered with her blood. "I guess that's it," he said. He drew his fingers across his face, looked at them and smiled at the blood he saw there.

BOLAN SAT in the Econolodge parking lot, fighting off drowsiness and feeling entirely useless. He should probably welcome the quiet break, but all that rest did for him was take the edge off, the edge that kept him alive in his constant flirtation with death.

He should never have let Brognola talk him into this, he thought. As he had explained to the Fed, the job was at odds with his principles. When you lay down with pigs you couldn't help but come away dirty, and Sam Giancarlo and his "family" were swine of the highest order. The old man's record of murder, prostitution, dope and loan-sharking went back all the way to the thirties and the criminal empire set up by Lucky Luciano. The price tag for the pain, suffering and degradation that this one man had caused was beyond calculation, and the thought of Giancarlo living out the rest of his life under sympathetic government supervision was almost more than the Executioner could bear.

He looked at his watch. He'd been sitting there in the motel parking lot for nearly two hours, two hours of wasted time and energy.

His rearview mirror suddenly glowed with lights as a car pulled up right behind. All senses went on full alert, one hand moved closer to the combat webbing he wore under his sport jacket.

He checked the sideview and saw the door of the car behind opening. Joan Meredith stepped out, her face strained, hard. Something was wrong.

He leaned across the seat and unlocked the door on the passenger side so she could get in. She sat beside him and looked straight ahead through the windshield.

"What happened?" he asked.

"Somebody hit Vito Perezzi tonight," she announced.

"When? Where?"

"About an hour ago in south L.A., Laguna Beach." She turned and looked at him. "They got him at home."

"This changes everything." Bolan rubbed his eyes. Both he and Brognola had hoped the Pallonatti hit was a fluke, with no connection to witness protection. But now it was obvious it was no fluke. He knew what came next.

"Yeah," she replied. "Our investigation has just gone out front and active."

"Hal sent you out here, didn't he?"

She stared at him for a moment, frowning. "I'm not going to pressure you, Mack, if that's what you're afraid of. I'd like to have you with me, but I understand your feelings on this."

"Give me the whole thing," he replied, turning in the seat to watch her.

She took a long breath. "Hal's had second thoughts," she said. "Perezzi's murder coming so soon after Pallonatti's makes him think they're going for a full-house sweep, and pretty fast . . ."

"I agree," Bolan said.

"Next, there's two options. Either gather up the rest of the witnesses and try to hide them, or send them protection right now for whatever happens."

"Let me guess," Bolan said. "The first option might not work, because they could be under surveillance already, plus they aren't going to want to move. But if we offer federal protection right on the spot, it might scare off the killers until they can arrange something more substantial."

"That was Hal's thought, too," Meredith replied.

"It's the next part I don't want to hear."

She narrowed her eyes. "Our investigations here will be handled through regular channels now. We're all being shipped out as bodyguards."

"We?" Bolan's tone was sharp.

"All of us . . . you, if you want to."

"I don't want to."

"I understand."

"Do you?"

"Look," she said. "Hal told me not to push you on this. I'll be in charge out there. Hal does ask that you stay here and supervise the surveillance. He thinks it's still important to locate the leak."

"I agree with that, too." Bolan hated the thought of sending his squad into action without him. He'd only known most of them for two days, but by God, they were *his* people. Again he damned his stupidity for getting into this situation. "Tell me exactly what happened."

"Not much to tell," she answered. "Perezzi and his wife were having dinner with a couple from farther down the beach. Apparently some gunmen interrupted their meal and blew them all away. Another neighbor heard screaming and called the police."

"Strange," Bolan mused. "It doesn't add up."

"What do you mean?"

"I've been studying the Mafia for many years," he said. "This doesn't fit the pattern. First of all, when they put a hit on someone, they try to do it where they can dispose of the body so it won't be found, the way they did with Pallonatti. They're always concerned about too much adverse publicity because it puts the heat on them. The second thing is sort of a personal scruple. Most Mafia hoods won't hit the victim's wife. That way his own wife won't get hit. It's kind of an unwritten law."

"What are you saying?" she asked.

"I think that whoever set up this killing went outside the family to get it taken care of," he said. "That's kind of scary, because it adds a wild card to the proceedings, an unexpected problem. This thing won't be resolved through regular channels only. Does Hal plan on taking any action on his suspects in the leak?"

"He's already gotten authorization to drag them all in for lie detector tests," she said.

"Good. Soon, I hope."

"Tomorrow morning."

This was going to be a messy one, Bolan thought, far messier than Joan Meredith realized. He forced himself to think about directly protecting Mafia scum, then pictured her lying on the floor somewhere with her head blown off because he wasn't around. He couldn't stand the first thought and couldn't live with the other.

"I want a video tape of the death scene," he said, "or at least photographs. We're going to need to be on this as early tomorrow as possible. How far apart are the three remaining men scattered?"

"They're all across the country," she said. "Does this mean you're going to go?"

He nodded curtly. "If you don't mind my taking your job?"

She leaned across the seat and hugged him. "I've never been so glad to be second fiddle in my life."

He returned the hug. It felt good, comfortable. "Let's get back now. We need to pull this together and make some decisions."

"What about your stakeout here?" she asked.

Bolan frowned. "Probably a late night card game or a liaison with a Senate page. The way the people in this town live, anything's possible."

She opened the car door and climbed out, then turned to address him. "Thanks, Mack. You're doing the right thing."

"I sure hope you know what you're talking about," he replied, starting the engine, "because every instinct in my body is screaming that I'm making a mistake."

"Don't worry, big guy." She smiled. "I'll protect you."

He put the car into gear. "See you back at base," he said as she shut the car door. Then he pulled away from the Econolodge, catching New York Avenue back toward the Capitol. Joan Meredith eased her car into the light evening traffic right behind him.

Had either of them looked into the rearview mirror when they were pulling out, they would have noticed a Justice Department lawyer named Ken Chasen and a woman known as Yvette pause arm in arm inside the glass double doors of the motel for a lingering kiss, before Chasen headed into the parking garage.

5

He had a pretrial this morning on, of all things, one of the Giancarlo indictments. Ken Chasen shook his head. It was Mann Act stuff involving the transportation of hookers from New York to Chicago, as if there weren't enough hookers in Chicago already.

The papers were rattling because of the tremor in his hands, and he had to set them down finally, and sit back to rub his eyes. He should have got more sleep last night; he shouldn't have had the fight with Marie when he got home from being with Yvette. He shouldn't have snorted almost three grams of coke during the course of the night, either, but it had been that kind of a night.

His eyes were red and swollen and his stomach hurt, and now this goddamn pretrial. He'd put off preparing it for weeks, such a minor indictment in the overall scheme of things, but now it was time and he was about halfway to hell.

The phone rang.

Oh, God, what now? He stared at the phone, not wanting to talk to anybody. It rang again. He put his hand on it, but didn't pick it up. After four rings it stopped and he took his hand off.

A man could take just so much pressure, and besides the job, there was the thing with Yvette. He had to break it off, had to forget the whole stupid business. If only...only...

"There you are." At the sound of the voice, he looked up. Kaminsky was standing in his doorway.

"I just called you," he said.

"You must have misdialed," Chasen told him. "Nothing rang in here."

"Is something wrong?" Kaminsky looked him over. "You don't look well."

"I'm...fine," Chasen answered, avoiding the man's eyes. "What's up?"

"Something ridiculous," Kaminsky said, shaking his head. "We're all going to have to take lie detector tests."

Chasen wanted to scream. "We're *what*?"

Kaminsky frowned. "Crazy, huh? Authorization came down this morning. They say it's just general security clearance checks, but I think it's got something to do with the Perezzi killing...you remember Perezzi?"

Chasen felt the life draining out of him. God, he thought, his information had killed Perezzi. Somehow he hadn't realized it would happen so soon, so...publicly. "What happened?"

"A bunch of guys gunned down Perezzi, his wife and another couple last night," Kaminsky said, moving up to sit on the edge of the desk. "Odd, isn't it?

That's usually not the Mafia's style. Anyway, I think they suspect there might be a relocation leak coming out of this department, especially coming so soon after the Pallonatti murder.''

Chasen fell back in his chair. "No one ever told me Pallonatti was murdered."

"We talked about it a couple of nights ago at Phillips," Kaminsky said. "Guess you weren't there." He looked at his watch. "Anyway, we're due down at the torture chamber in about ten minutes."

"I can't go," Chasen said, looking around his desk as if he'd lost something. "I've got a pretrial at ten. I've got to prepare."

The older man stood and walked to the door, pausing with his hand on the knob. "This is priority, pal. The pretrial will have to wait. Coming?"

"No," Chasen said, his insides jangling. "You go ahead. I'll be right along."

Kaminsky shrugged and closed the door, leaving Chasen sitting like a statue, frozen in panic. It had never occurred to him that he would be faced with the consequences of his illegal action on this, that he would have to live with blood, innocent blood, on his hands. It had all seemed so easy, just hand over a piece of paper and everything would be all right. It was just paper, paper with a few scribbled words on it. Now, everything seemed so final, so irredeemable.

What was he going to do? He could never pass a lie detector test about a relocation leak. Trading off those names and addresses in violation of law was bad enough, but now the charge was conspiracy to commit murder and accessory before and after the fact. The loss of his career paled in comparison to the years he would spend in jail—and that was if he didn't get the death penalty. It wasn't fair.

If only he could think straight. It was so quiet, the offices already empty around him, even the receptionist's constantly humming radio turned off. He looked at the phone. Yvette. He'd call Yvette. She'd know what to do.

He ripped the phone off the switchhook and punched up the Econolodge numbers with a trembling finger. "Five-eighteen, please," he said when they answered.

"I'm sorry, sir," a woman's voice answered. "There is no one registered in 518."

"But the young lady..."

"There was a lady registered there," the hotel operator said, "but she checked out last night."

"Checked out," Chasen repeated. "Are you absolutely..."

"Is there something else I can help you with?" she asked.

For some reason that struck Chasen as funny. He laughed as he hung up the phone, laughter that turned quickly to tears of self-pity. What was he going to do? If only he wasn't so dragged out. If only he could think straight. He needed something to clear his mind, to straighten him out.

He knew what to do.

He reached into his suit coat pocket and pulled out the small silver vial. He had promised himself that he'd save this for after work, but he really needed it now. Just a little something to help his thought processes, that was all.

He locked the door of his office, then hurried back to the desk and, with mounting excitement, cleared a spot on its glass surface.

A razor blade lay amid the pile of white powder inside the vial. He used the edge of the blade to scoop out several little mounds of coke and lay them carefully on the desktop. Then he used the blade to chop up the crystal chunks into a fine powder and spread it out into three long lines.

He pulled a twenty-dollar bill out of his pocket and rolled it into a small tube. He stared at the drug, amazed at how badly he wanted it. Leaning down, he pushed the end of the paper tube into one nostril and snorted up the first two lines. He sat back, waiting for the familiar rush of numbness to settle him down.

It came on quickly, calming him somewhat, at least for the moment. His mind cleared. He could think again. He looked at the third line. What the hell! He leaned down and snorted it, too, then with a forefinger picked up the dust left on the desktop to spread on his gums.

So, what was done was done. He couldn't bring those dead people back. What he needed to do was cover his own ass. Where was Yvette? Why had she left? He looked at his watch. He needed to get downstairs quickly. But how? How could he get through the lie detector test?

And then he remembered. One of his witness relocation people had once told him of a way to beat the system. Working quickly he pulled off his right shoe and sock. Hurrying now, he pulled open his desk drawer and sorted through it until he came out with a thumbtack and a small dispenser of tape.

He carefully snugged the tack up against his big toe with the point just sticking him. Then he taped it in that position and very slowly put his sock back on, flinching every time he pulled too hard. The shoe came next with similar results.

He stood up, so stoned he felt straight, and made his way through the offices to the elevator. He had to walk slowly to keep the tack from digging painfully into him. Lie detectors were not really lie detectors at all. They were machines designed to measure emotional responses to questions, and if the emotions could be thrown off during the questioning, so could the results.

Kaminsky was just coming out of interrogation when Chasen walked into the waiting room where the rest of his co-workers were already awaiting their turn.

"Doesn't hurt a bit," Kaminsky said, smiling, then added, "You're next because of the timing of the pre-trial."

Chasen nodded, still averting his eyes. He floated into interrogation on a cloud, feeling somehow insulated from everything around him.

The technician directed him to a chair with wires on it in the middle of the sparsely furnished room. When he sat down, the man strapped electrodes to his head, chest and arms.

"Okay, Mr. Chasen," the technician said, going to the control board. "First thing we need to do is establish a control sector. I'm going to ask you a number of simple questions. Either lie or tell the truth, it doesn't matter. We're simply setting some bottom limits on the scale. Understood?"

Chasen nodded.

"Okay," the man said. "Your name is Bozo the Clown, correct?"

Chasen kicked the chair leg, driving the tack painfully into his toe. "Correct," he said.

"Your wife's name is Marie."

He kicked the chair again. "Correct."

"You have fifteen children."

Same procedure. "Correct," he said, fighting off waves of pain.

"Mr. Chasen," the man asked, "you don't need to tell me any details but I have to ask if you've been having any emotional problems lately? Your readings are extremely high."

"I, uh, had a fight with my wife last night," Chasen answered, "and I didn't get much sleep as a result."

"Well, I guess you're just an excitable person." The technician picked up a pen as he leaned over the scrolling graph. "Okay. Let's continue. You've worked for the Justice Department for ten years?"

He kicked the chair, his toe agonizing fire. "Correct."

"You have a top-secret security clearance?"

"Correct."

"Have you ever misused your clearance in any way?"

He backed off from the tack, the pain subsiding considerably. "No. Absolutely not."

"Have you ever had occasion to access the closed files containing the whereabouts of individuals protected under witness relocation?"

"No. Never."

"Have you ever given, or allowed to be given, any information from the closed files to any unauthorized person either within the government infrastructure or outside of it?"

He dwelt on the subsiding pain in his toe, letting his mind drift away from the subject. He felt ethereal, like a floating cloud, totally disassociated. "No," he said.

The technician looked at the results, running the graph back to check previous high points for several long agonizing minutes before shrugging and saying, "Looks like a clean bill of health, Mr. Chasen. But I'd advise you to work harder on getting along with your wife."

Chasen forced a smile. "Thanks." He got up and walked out the door, down the hall and into the men's room, where he cried for fifteen minutes before he was able to get himself together enough to return to his desk.

As ROY CARVER DROVE, Bolan looked again at a photograph of the interrupted party at Laguna Beach, food and broken glass strewn carelessly around the dead. He had been through a stack of 8 x 10s similar to this one several times, all to the same result: he was more convinced than ever that the slaughter was an outside job—a fact that he couldn't reconcile with the vendettalike nature of the killings.

"I've never seen so many pickup trucks," Carver said as he wheeled the car through the southside streets of Oklahoma City. They had rented the Chevy at Will Rogers Airport and driven straight here, looking for Old Sam Giancarlo's house. "And they've all got guns in the back window."

"Yeah," Bolan replied. "Guns are a large component of life here. Old Sam must feel right at home. Once we crossed the South Canadian River a while back we entered what's called Cow Town or Packing Town, where the slaughterhouses and meat packers are."

"Just like Chicago," Carver said.

"Yeah."

Bolan put away the photographs and watched the post-World War II frame housing slide by. Giancarlo had settled here after trying out living in a couple of larger cities; to Bolan, his final choice of oil-busted Oklahoma City to settle reflected a mind that was tired and wanted nothing more than rest. Old Sam was weary. Bolan figured that was the principal reason why he had chosen to sell out the other families and run away.

Bolan had dispatched the other members of his squad to protect the Giancarlo clan members in Seattle and Denver. He had chosen to watch Giancarlo himself; Old Sam's testimony was potentially the most damaging because it was firsthand, not hearsay; this made him the most likely target. The man was willing to testify to direct involvement by the other families in illegal enterprises, something that, as Brognola had said, could literally break the hold of the Mob in Chicago. But given that fact, why had Pallonatti and Perezzi been wasted first? It seemed logical for the most dangerous man to be killed first, before protective steps were taken or even thought necessary. There were so many things that didn't add up with this deal, so much still to put together.

"Are we going to meet another security team at Giancarlo's house?" Carver asked, his eyes moving rapidly between the road and the Oklahoma City Mapsco in his lap.

"We're it," Bolan said. "What do you want, gift wrapping?"

"Are you serious?" Carver asked, turning to give the big man an inquiring look. "You saw those pictures. It looks like there are a bunch of them...."

"I figure three or four." Bolan met Carver's stare. "Look...what can we do? There are literally thousands of people on witness protection, and as much as we'd like to believe we know who the targets are on this thing, the fact is we can't be sure, at least not sure enough to convince the powers that be that what's needed now is a large investment of manpower."

"What about the lie detector tests?" Carver turned the car onto a north-south street with the ambiguous name of Western Avenue.

Bolan showed empty palms. "The tests came out clean—no leaks at Justice."

"You believe that?"

"No," Bolan replied. "But what are we going to do? With nothing more to go on than what we've got, there's just no chance of prying loose more personnel from Justice or anywhere else. To make a long story short, the buck stops with us."

"Anything on the other dead people in Laguna Beach?"

Bolan nodded, remembering the photos. "The other couple were a doctor and his wife from down the beach. It was clean . . . just friends having dinner together. Perezzi used to run Old Sam's legitimate businesses for him. Most of his friends were from the civilian community."

"God, those people don't screw around, do they?" Carver asked.

Bolan shrugged. He couldn't argue with Carver's assessment.

"This doesn't make any sense," Carver continued. "I'd feel really stupid getting killed while defending the kind of dude I joined Enforcement to stop."

Bolan ignored the statement. He couldn't argue with it, either. Instead he turned to catch the hundred block on the corner street sign. The neighborhood had gotten progressively better the farther they'd driven, until now they were passing large barnlike houses of brick and siding. "I think we're about two blocks from our turnoff," he said. "What's the name of the area?"

"Willow Run." Carver frowned. "What's the deal on witness protection, anyway? Maybe I'd like to go into a life of crime."

"Basically, the government sets you up," Bolan replied, "gives you a new name, gets you work if you need it and pays you a monthly stipend. The amount and the size of the stipend, of course, are determined by how much help the witness gives the government. Look, there's your turn."

Carver drove into the Willow Run neighborhood. Its sign and outer fence were badly in need of repair. As Carver got closer to Giancarlo's house, Bolan's spirits sank. He had prepared himself intellectually to deal with the Mafia head, but as they got physically closer, he was getting all churned up emotionally.

Most of the houses they were passing either had For Sale signs on them or were empty. The neighborhood appeared to be eighty percent vacant, a symptom of Oklahoma's hard times since the crash of '81 destroyed the state's single-resource economy. Such low occupancy made for a bad killzone. There were too many places to hide.

As if echoing his thoughts, Carver remarked, "This would be a hellhole to defend. Why don't we take the old man someplace else?"

"He won't leave his home. He says Villani never scared him off before and he won't now."

"Great."

"Willow Way." Bolan pointed to a street sign. "Take a right. He should be on the cul-de-sac."

The street was only one block long, and Giancarlo's house was at the dead end, directly facing and cutting off the road with its commanding presence. A ten-year-old black Lincoln was parked in the driveway next to a Camaro convertible. Giancarlo's new name, Smithfield, was printed on the streetside mailbox.

Carver pulled up behind the Lincoln, and both men got out of the car. The weather was still warm, and Bolan wished he'd worn a short-sleeved shirt under his sport jacket. "Should we take our bags in?" Carver asked.

"Better see what kind of reception we get first."

Bolan knocked at the door of the two-story brick dwelling, his eyes roving the neighboring houses and landscape around them for anything out of the ordinary. Several houses on the cul-de-sac appeared empty.

"Does he have a job?" Carver asked, after a minute passed and no sound was heard.

"Old Sam? I don't know," Bolan said. "They wouldn't give me access to his file, just his address."

"He is expecting us, isn't he?"

"I'm sure Hal—"

"Freeze!" someone behind them screamed. Bolan instinctively dived sideways, coming up with Big Thunder.

"Justice Department!" Bolan yelled as he watched the man training a .38 on Carver. "Drop the weapon."

"*You* drop it or your buddy dies." The man cocked the hammer and moved up to stick the barrel into Carver's throat. "Drop it now!"

Bolan stood, raising his own aim to the man's head. "You do what you want," he said calmly. "The choice is yours. But if you choose to kill that man, you won't live long enough to make other choices. My name's Belasko and this is my partner, Carver. Hal Brognola has sent us down as protection from the Justice Department. Mr. Carver is going to reach slowly into his sport jacket and take out his identification. It's your choice."

"Don't move."

"Do it," Bolan said, moving several steps closer to the man, holding his gun outstretched, two-handed.

As Carver raised a hand to his inner breast pocket his assailant didn't move, didn't flinch—but he didn't shoot, either. Carver got into his pocket without incident, brought out his ID and handed it to the gunman.

The man glanced quickly at the badge, then backed up a pace, lowering the long-barrel .38. "My name's Joey Giancarlo," he said, turning to glare at Bolan, who was still aiming his weapon at the man's head.

"Prove it," Bolan said. "Roy. Get the gun."

Carver removed the .38 from the man's hand, then grabbed the wallet out of his pocket.

"You son of a bitch," the man said. He was young, in his twenties, and looked like a hothead. "I'll get you for this."

"He's Joey Giancarlo, all right." Carver showed Bolan the wallet. A new driver's license had his new name, but he still carried old ID and club cards in the name Giancarlo.

"Well, so he is," Bolan replied. He lowered the gun.

Joey snapped the wallet out of Carver's hand. "Fuckin' cops are all alike," he said, then smiled. "So you guys are my hired hands." His smile turned to a laugh.

"What's so funny?" Carver said.

Joey Giancarlo shook his head. "Nothin'," he said. "Nothin's funny. Come on around back, I'll introduce you to my old man."

Bolan and Carver followed Joey around the side of the house. It was a large, relatively new place, one that would sell for close to a half million on the coast, but that was probably worth less than a hundred thousand in Oklahoma's economy. Even at that, he was sure that Old Sam could afford much better. Like most mafiosi, he had to protect his real income, his blood money, from prying government eyes.

The old man sat in the middle of the backyard, weeding out the last of the brown summer grass from a garden and preparing for fall planting. He had aged considerably since the last picture Bolan had seen of him was taken, but when he looked up, his strong, cruel eyes bored into Bolan, and his face wore a tight-lipped sneer. He was still the *padrone*.

"Hey," Joey said, still smiling. "Look at our new boys—the G-men they sent down from witness protection."

Giancarlo stood, carefully removing his gardening gloves and folding them before setting them on the small stool he had used for a seat amid the weeds and dead flowers. He looked at Joey. "Go get me a cold drink," he said without inflection.

He walked out of the garden slowly, staring intently at Bolan the whole time. "You can't grow nothin' here," he said. "The whole place is damned red clay. They give it ta the Indians because it wasn't worth nothin' for farmin'. Then they discover the oil and send the Indians off someplace else. You're a killer, ain't you?"

"My name's Belasko," Bolan said. "They don't pay me enough to give you any more than that."

Giancarlo pointed a crooked finger at him. "You're a killer for sure. And you hate my guts."

"I hate more than your guts," Bolan replied.

The man grinned, revealing toothless gums. "I like that," he said. "You hate me 'cause I break the law, huh? 'Cause I sell poor people numbers and lend people money when they can't get it no place else."

Giancarlo put his hand on his chest and tapped it. "My damn heart bleeds for you, killer. I'm just a man that looks out for his family, that's all, a family man."

Bolan just stared at him, the man returning the stare in full measure, enjoying the game.

"Tell me, killer," Giancarlo said, "who's the coon with you?"

Bolan's eyes widened and he turned quickly to Carver, who stood with clenched fists and dark eyes. "This is my associate, Mr. Carver."

"Well, you associate with whoever you want," Old Sam stated, "but ain't no jungle bunny comin' into my house."

"We're a package," Bolan said, turning to stare Carver to silence. "You get us both or nothing."

Giancarlo pursed his lips, wrinkling his face like a raisin. "He don't eat with the rest of us. There's a servant room off the kitchen he can sleep in."

"Neither one of us wants to eat with you," Bolan returned. "As for that servant's room, it sounds perfect for both of us. And I'll tell you something else. I almost can hope I fail, because guys like you deserve killing."

Giancarlo threw back his head and laughed loudly, slapping his leg. "I know you too good, government killer. You'd let 'em get you before they get me, huh? Same with the black boy who can't eat at my table. Well, don't you worry. Benito Villani is an oily old dago who tried his whole life to get the better of me. So, you kill Villani for me and maybe I move back to Chicago. What do you say?"

Bolan made no reply, for the sound of a noisy argument caught the attention of all three. Bolan reached for Big Thunder, as Joey Giancarlo and a young woman with long, black hair came around the corner of the house. The woman had a definite uptown look to her, her clothes well tailored and stylish, her face beautiful despite being twisted as she expressed vehement disagreement with Joey. Joey broke away from her and hurried over to the old man.

"I told her." He spread his arms and showed empty palms. "I told her it wasn't safe and she should go someplace else...."

"Daddy!" the woman cried, running to the old man and kissing him on the cheek. "I heard about Uncle Rico and Mr. Perezzi on the radio. I was so worried."

"I'm real glad to see you, baby." Giancarlo hugged the woman to him, then pulled away. "But you don't want to be around here now."

"Nonsense! If there's some sort of trouble I want to be with you."

"That's the worst thing you could do," Bolan told her.

The young woman looked at him, eyes flashing. "And who the hell are you?" she asked harshly.

"Angela," Old Sam said, "this is Mr. Belasko and Mr. Carver, his...partner. The government sent them down to look out for me. So you see? Everything's okay here. You go back to Los Angeles and write good stories for your movies. I'll be fine."

"Sorry, Daddy," she said, "but I'm not leaving as long as there's trouble. I can write here just as well as in L.A. Maybe you can send one of these gentlemen to carry in my bags for me."

Giancarlo looked at Bolan. "You see, killer? You see how my family loves me?"

"Miss Giancarlo," Bolan said. "If you truly want to help your father, then staying here is not the way to do it. There are only two of us here to protect—"

"Three," Joey interrupted.

"Three," Bolan repeated. "And if we have to divide our time between your father *and* you, I'm afraid we won't be nearly as effective."

"Why don't you just arrest Ben Villani?" she said. "He's the one behind all this."

"We don't have any direct evidence linking Villani with the murders," Bolan said. "But in any case, for your father's safety I insist you turn right around and take the next plane to Los Angeles, if that's where you make your home."

She stared hard at Bolan, her eyes liquid brown pools, her face smooth as olive oil, then turned to Giancarlo. "What do you want me to do, Daddy?"

"It won't be safe for you here, honey," he said. "I'm tired. I ain't gonna run from Ben no more. Maybe these fellas can help me out, but if you're here..."

Angela Giancarlo nodded, kissing her father on the cheek again. "I'll leave," she said, "but I won't go to Los Angeles. I'll check into a motel or something under a different name. That's safe enough, isn't it?"

Bolan nodded. He knew that was the best he was going to get from her.

"Good," she said. "That way we can visit, and you can show me your new home."

"You're a good girl, Angie," Old Sam said. "Your mama woulda been proud of you."

As the two walked arm in arm into the house, Bolan tried to figure out how such an open sewer as Sam Giancarlo could have produced such refinement and beauty.

"THE FOOD WAS FINE," Ken Chasen said irritably. "I just wasn't hungry, that's all."

He scraped another plate and handed it to Marie, who put it in the dishwasher. "You hardly eat anymore," she complained. "You're getting thin. It's probably why you're getting so hard to get along with."

"Great!" he said loudly. "Now I'm hard to get along with." He picked up another plate, but it slipped through his fingers and crashed to the floor.

"Shit!"

Two-year-old Billy came charging into the kitchen. "Daddy break! Daddy break!"

Chasen glared down at the child, angry and frustrated. "Would you shut up?" he yelled. "You're always underfoot, always nagging...."

Shocked by his father's tone more than by his words, the boy backed away, crying loudly.

"Leave him alone!" Marie cried, bending to hug the child to her. She looked up at Chasen in fear and horror. "What's wrong with you? What in God's name has happened?"

"Nothing's happened." He glowered at her, disgusted by the sickening show she was putting on with the baby. "I'm just sick of you. I'm sick to death of all of this!"

He picked up another plate, smashing it into the sink, then another, and another. With each crash Billy cried louder.

"Stop it!" Marie screamed. "Oh God!"

With a loud groan, Chasen charged out of the room and locked himself in the master bathroom. He leaned against the washstand on stiffened arms, looking at the red-eyed madman who stared back at him from the mirror.

Damn Marie and her foolishness! Damn her for not trying to understand him! Where the hell was Yvette? She'd know what to say, what to do. How could she just leave like that without leaving a message for him . . . something? And on top of everything else, he was sure that Bert Kaminsky was watching him. Nothing ever slid by that son of a bitch. Easygoing old Bert had a suspicious legal mind. He probably had the whole thing figured out.

Chasen opened the vanity cabinet doors. Way in the back of a shelf was a box of cotton swabs. He dumped out the package off white-tipped wooden sticks on the countertop, and picked up the plastic bag of coke he had stashed beneath the swabs.

The bag was weighty, reassuring. There was still plenty there, enough to last him a long time. But Yvette was his only source. What if he couldn't find her? He couldn't possibly face life without her *and* without cocaine.

He poured a generous amount of coke onto the countertop, then used a credit card from his wallet to divide it into two lines. Bending down, he snorted up the big lines using the cut-off plastic straw he kept in his pocket. He hadn't slept for two days now, his euphoria having taken on a harder, more demanding edge. But things were so out of control that he didn't see any way of coping other than increasing his cocaine use.

As the anesthetic calmed his brain, he heard the ring of the bedroom telephone extension just outside the bathroom. He ignored it, assuming Marie would answer the phone. The coke had gone down so well that he poured out a little more onto the countertop. He had just lined it up with the plastic card and was bending to snort it when Marie came into the bedroom.

"Ken . . ." she called through the locked door.

"Not now." He eased the straw up his nose and ingested half the line.

"You're wanted on the phone, Ken."

"I told you, not now!" He drew the rest of the line into his other nostril.

"She says it's urgent . . . someone named Yvette."

"I'll be right there," he said.

Frantically he dropped the coke back into its hiding place, awkwardly scooping the cotton swabs back into the box before tossing it to the back of the shelf where he kept it. Remembering just in time to wipe the residual powder off his nose and upper lip, he turned and opened the door.

Marie stood staring at him. "Who's Yvette?" she asked.

"Just somebody I work with." He brushed past her.

"I've never heard of—"

"Get off my back, will you?" he snapped, and hurried into his study, locking the door behind him.

The phone was inside his rolltop desk. He pulled back the accordion door and grabbed the receiver. "Don't talk yet," he warned, then put his hand over the mouthpiece. "I've got it now!" A second later he heard the other line hang up.

"Okay," he said into the phone. "It's clear."

"Oh darling, is that you?" Yvette almost sobbed. "I've been so worried, so..."

"Where are you? I've been frantic. They made us all take lie detector tests this morning at work."

"Did you take one?"

"Where are you?" he asked again. "I can't be away from you like this. I'm going nuts."

"They made me leave," she explained. "God, I didn't want to. They made me talk to them, made me tell them that you'd continue to work with them on this..."

"What do you mean, continue?" He began to feel queasy in the stomach. "You told me that it was all over, that when I gave them the paper and you gave me that tape..."

"They've got another tape, Ken. They want to make sure the job is carried out to completion. I'm so sorry. What about the lie detector test?"

"I think I got through it," he said, "but I have a feeling my supervisor suspects something. I've got to see you. I can't hold together like this."

"Are they taking any other steps?" she asked.

"I—I don't know. Please, I must see you," he begged.

"I'm in Chicago, I don't—"

"Tell them that if I don't see you alone, I'll blow the whole thing apart. I mean it, Yvette. I'm going crazy."

"Listen," she said. "Do you remember where we went that first night?"

"Sure, I..."

"Shh. Don't say it. I'll meet you there at midnight tomorrow. But you must be prepared to update my information." She sounded frightened. "It's the only way, my love."

"Okay," he promised. "I'll do it."

"Until tomorrow, then." She hung up.

He stood there, feeling the room closing in on him. After all he'd gone through they wanted more. And Yvette, poor Yvette, whose only crime was loving her brother, was caught in the middle. He'd get money, that was what he'd do. He'd find enough money to spring Yvette out of this mess and to safety.

"Ken?" Marie was knocking hesitantly on the door. "Is everything all right?"

God, she was getting on his nerves. Couldn't a man have any peace? He walked over and threw open the door. "What?" he demanded.

She had a resolute look on her face, as if she'd reached some major determination. "Something's wrong," she said. "I know it is. Please tell me about it. I'm your wife, I..."

"Wrong!" he screamed, seizing her around the neck. "You want to know what's wrong?" Still grabbing her throat, he shook her, banged her head against the wall. "You're what's wrong! You keep pushing me. Pushing...pushing..."

She was gagging, her eyes wide and frightened, her fingers trying to loosen the unrelenting pressure of his grasp. He felt nothing, but when her eyelids began fluttering, he released her. She fell to the floor, gasping for breath.

"See what you made me do?" he asked calmly. "You just don't know when to stop."

She climbed to her knees, still coughing, her face twisted in a grimace of disgust and fear that he was sure she had rehearsed just for his benefit. She staggered to her feet and ran out of the room without a word.

He stood there, shaking his head. The stupid bitch! She had pushed him to that with her prying and poking around. Yvette would never do that to him. Not Yvette.

He walked to his desk, sat in the executive chair Marie had given him for Christmas three years previously. In the top desk drawer lay the video tape that had been made of him and Yvette as they snorted coke and made passionate love. Just holding the tape aroused his desire for the woman. In some perverse way, he was proud of the tape, proud of his virility.

He heard a car in the driveway and hurried to the window. Marie had gathered up the children and put them in the car. She was backing out, going—where?

He didn't care. Good riddance. He didn't need the bitch, anyway. He stood alone . . . in control.

6

Carol Niven stood in the hall, watching Barberi as he slowly packed his bags, talking to himself all the while. The old man was half blind. It seemed somehow incongruous to her that the government would waste time, money and personnel to protect someone like him.

Barberi had spent the past three hours telling them how in his youth he'd been the greatest wheelman in the business, recounting stories that, if they hadn't gotten better with age, should have been in the *Guinness Book of World Records*. He had spent most of the afternoon trying to decide whether to stay or "take it on the lam," as he liked to say, finally deciding that discretion was the better part of valor. He had even told them—five times—the story of how he'd got the nickname, Stinky. The name referred to the smell of the grease he'd used to slick down his hair when he was young—when he'd had hair. Sam Giancarlo had first called him Stinky in 1934, and the nickname had stuck ever since. For some reason, that fact was important to him.

Life had changed a lot since Stinky had been running loose on the streets. Niven's training reflected that. It was geared as much toward psychology as to self-defense. But the old man had lost none of his arrogance and selfish stupidity. Perhaps, to Stinky, it was still 1934.

She turned and walked back to the tiny kitchen, where her partner, Lomax, was peering out the window, a coffee cup in his hand.

"Looks like he's just about ready," she said.

Lomax turned abruptly, nearly spilling his coffee. "Who's nervous...not me," he joked, wiping a few drops off his wrist. "I wish to God he'd made his decision to leave three hours ago."

"Did you see something?" she asked.

He sat down at the small kitchen table. "Just dark...shadows...my mind weirding out. I don't know. This whole thing gives me the creeps. Did you find a hotel?"

"Yeah," she replied as she, too, sat. She stared at the red-checked tablecloth. "We're in at the Red Lion Sea-Tac."

"How many rooms?" Lomax wiggled his eyebrows in a Groucho Marx imitation.

"I got a suite. Plenty of room for all three of us, and no, Neal, you're not going to get lucky tonight."

"If you were as freaked out as I am," he replied, "getting lucky would be about the last thing on your mind."

She smiled at him. "Then I guess I'm as freaked out as you are."

"First real assignment?"

She nodded, her own apprehensions growing in proportion to the deepening darkness.

"Me, too," he said. "I hope it's a quiet one."

"Well, come on." Barberi stormed into the room with a pasteboard suitcase swinging in his hand. "Let's clear out of here before it gets too late."

Lomax and Niven stood, then Niven checked the load on the .45 in her purse. "I'll take a look outside first," she said as she snapped the clip back into the butt of the weapon.

"Pretty big gun for such a little lady," Barberi commented, scratching his head through the wisps of white hair. "Back in my day..."

"I know," she said. "The women only shot off their mouths."

"Yeah." The old man cackled. "Shooting was something the men did, if you know what I mean?" He leered at Niven. "If you want, I'll show you later at the hotel."

"No thanks," she told him. "I'm on duty, remember?"

She walked from the kitchen to the small living room, where she retrieved her quilted jacket from a chair back. The house was poorly furnished and had the unpleasant smell of poverty and dirt. Apparently Barberi was living completely on government subsidy, having saved nothing from his years of crime. After all, the proceeds from illegal activities were not pensionable earnings.

She turned out the living room light and moved cautiously to the front door, opening it a crack. The night was as dark as any she'd ever seen; whatever moon there was was totally obscured by the cloud cover characteristic of Seattle, where it rains 258 days a year. It was downright cold tonight, a light drizzle slicking over everything, forming the barest skim of ice on the porch steps.

There were three steps down to the tiny, fenced yard. Niven kept her purse wrapped against her chest, her right hand inside the purse, holding the automatic.

The neighborhood was one of small, tar paper or frame one-story houses, near Meadow Point. As in most working-class neighborhoods, cars were parked everywhere—some old, in various stages of renovation, repair or decay, others, incongruously, new and fancy.

She was glad they were finally getting on the road, for defense would be tough in this locale. She noticed a white Cadillac parked about a block away that she didn't remember seeing earlier, but it didn't seem like anything out of the ordinary for Meadow Point.

"Okay?" Lomax called from the front door.

"It's okay," she said, turning from side to side, making one last sweep. "Bring him out."

"WHO THE HELL'S THE BITCH, man?" Cleavon Brown asked as he looked through the binoculars at the woman on the front lawn of the pigeon's house.

"I don't know. If I didn't know better I'd say she was doing point recon." Burnett stretched out a hand for the field glasses. "Would you give me the glasses?"

"Just a minute," Cleavon said.

"Give me the fucking glasses!" Burnett demanded. "Whose do you think they are, anyway? Don't you be pulling any stunts with my stuff like you did with the walkie-talkie."

"Can't we turn on the heater?" Coolie asked from the back seat. "It's cold as a witch's teat back here."

"We don't want to overheat the car." Burnett finally wrested the binoculars away from Cleavon and raised them to his eyes.

"You're a fool, man," Cleavon said. "This is a goddamn Caddie. It ain't gonna overheat."

"Go to hell!" Burnett returned, staring at the woman through the glasses. It almost looked as if she had a gun in the purse. Was it possible their strike was expected? It had never occurred to him that they wouldn't have surprise on their side, that a linkage of the early victims on the hit list could warn the others to prepare for a hit. That changed things a lot. Why hadn't Jericho told him about that possibility?

"I'm cold, too," Juke chimed in from the back.

Sighing, Burnett reached down and started the car, the two men in the back cheering. "They're coming out," he said. "Get ready to roll. I think they're going off in the car."

"How many?" Coolie asked.

"Two plus the old man," Burnett answered. "And he's got a suitcase. I think the first two are armed, maybe all three."

"What kind of shit is this?" Cleavon exclaimed. "I signed on to plug a few white boys, not get involved in some war. How come you didn't tell us there'd be shooters?"

Burnett put down the glasses. "Because I didn't know, all right?"

"You some dumb son of a bitch, Burnett." Cleavon laughed. "Lordy, I don't know when I've seen nobody dumb as you."

"Shut up," Burnett rasped. "You shut up or I'll fuckin' kill you myself."

Cleavon grabbed Burnett by the shoulders, bringing their faces close together. "You just come on anytime you want, you skinheaded asshole. I'll lay your ass out like poured cement."

"They're leaving." Coolie pointed at the Barberi house. "What do we do?"

"We follow," Burnett told him, dropping the Cadillac into gear. "We'll either take them on the road, or when they hole up for the night."

"Maybe they ain't holing up," Cleavon suggested. "Maybe they gonna drive straight through for a Florida vacation."

"You don't like it, get out and move on," Burnett said.

"I would except that I wanna see how bad you can screw up before this is done," Cleavon said, testing how far he could push the other man.

Burnett just gave him a look and pulled away from the curb, following the Ford Escort wagon driven by one of the bodyguards. He kept an easy distance, the rain and darkness providing natural cover. He wasn't quite sure what to think about the turn of events. Maybe the people with the old man were always with him. Maybe their presence was routine, didn't mean anything. Anyway, with all the money Jericho was paying, it probably didn't matter. This was Burnett's big chance for a way out and up in life, and for all the money he was being paid, he'd go after his marks even if they had an army protecting them.

As much as Burnett hated to admit it to himself, Cleavon had struck a nerve when he'd speculated on a long trip. He wasn't going to tell the others unless he had to, but he hadn't thought to fill the gas tank lately and they were sitting on less than a quarter of a tank, which, he had already discovered, didn't go very far in a Caddie. He'd have to find a way to make the hit before he ran out of gas.

The Escort rumbled through the city proper, just edging the newly renovated harbor area of Puget Sound. The piers and shops that were so bright and colorful in the daytime were just drab shapes on a night that reduced everything to slick shades of gray and black. With the Cadillac still following discreetly, the wagon turned north, climbing one of the seven large hills upon which Seattle was built.

Burnett kept a block length between his car and the Escort. He had put aside the problems that had plagued him earlier and had lapsed into daydreams as Juke hummed tunelessly in the back. He smiled at the big man's musical attempts, knowing they had to be driving Cleavon crazy but that even Cleavon had more sense than to make Juke mad.

Cleavon was Burnett's worst problem now, he realized. From the start the man had simply refused to take Burnett's leadership seriously, had criticized and scoffed at his preparations and plans. Cleavon stayed around because of the money, but the pay was only enough to buy his presence, not his loyalty. Burnett had briefly considered offering the man more, but dismissed the idea, unable to bring himself to placate an asshole like Cleavon. Besides, a man like Cleavon Brown wasn't smart enough to survive a tough firefight for too long. Burnett found that thought reassuring.

They had driven through the heart of the city, passing the entrances to the old, underground city that had been rebuilt because of plumbing problems and were moving through the outskirts when Cleavon pointed through the rain-spotted windshield.

"They's pullin' over," he said, "the lot beside that liquor store."

Burnett checked the gas gauge and breathed a sigh of relief. "We'll take them here," he said.

"Yeah." Cleavon reached under the front seat and pulled out a riot gun.

"WE REALLY SHOULDN'T be doing this," Lomax told Barberi over his shoulder. "Why can't we wait until you're settled—"

"Because I told you, shit-for-brains, that the hootch stores won't be open by the time we get settled in,"

Barberi said. "And I'll be damned if I'm goin' through a night with you clowns without a drink. Look, there's a place. Pull over."

Lomax looked at Carol Niven. She wished someone with more experience was with them to tell them what was expected and what wasn't. "If we don't do it," she said, "he'll drive us crazy all night."

"Good point." Lomax turned on the blinker and talked over his shoulder. "If you know what you want, get it quick," he told Barberi. "Things are awfully exposed here."

Niven checked the parking lot as they approached. The package store, called Gambino's, was the corner building, brightly lit with yellow neon, the only place still open in a small business block. Lomax parked the wagon between two cars, and the three of them got out.

"Hey, I came away without any cash." Stinky patted his pockets like an expert. "Would you lend me a few..."

Frowning, Lomax reached into his pocket and fished out a ten-dollar-bill. "This is going to look good on the expense report," he remarked to Niven.

They walked into the store, where a young man sat reading a magazine behind a small counter jammed with candy and cigarettes. His eyes just touched them as they walked in the door before flicking to the big clock on the wall that read 9:27.

It was a medium-size place that used every available inch of space. Floor-to-ceiling shelves were filled with bottles of wine and liquor, with narrow aisles between.

While Barberi moved over to the display of cheap vodka, Carol Niven wandered over near the check-out stand where she could keep an eye on the parking lot.

"Can I help you?" asked the blond kid behind the counter.

"In a minute." Niven smiled, as she watched a white Cadillac that had just pulled into the parking lot. Hadn't she seen a car like that back in Barberi's neighborhood? But of course there were more than two white Cadillacs on the streets of Seattle. Her senses were tingling a warning, but she shut it off, not wanting to make a foolish rookie mistake her first night on the job.

She turned to the counter. "Can I have a Milky Way?" she asked the blonde.

BURNETT PULLED UP just around the corner of the building, in its side parking lot. He turned in the seat to address the others. "I'm going to go in and check it out," he said. "When I'm sure everything's okay inside, I'll come back out. We'll wait out here and hit 'em when they leave."

"What about the dude running the register?" Coolie asked.

"We'll have to hit him, too," Burnett replied.

"Look, man," Cleavon suggested as Coolie passed Burnett a shotgun over the seat. "We gotta off the dude in there anyway. Why not just go in and finish them off inside, then we can clean out the register, too, and make a few bucks.''

"Yeah,'' Juke said. "Maybe we can git a bottle of somethin' while we're there.''

"There's too much cover inside,'' Burnett told them as he turned off the dome light. "We need 'em in the open. We might be able to take the witness out right through the window.'' He opened the car door and climbed out. "Be right back.''

He shoved his hands in his pockets and walked into the store, walking up to the cash register with a smile on his face. The bitch was standing near the doorway unwrapping a candy bar, while a blond-haired punk ogled her from behind the counter.

"Help you?'' the kid asked.

"You got pints back there?'' Burnett asked.

"What do you need?''

"Whiskey, cheap as you got.''

He noticed the woman watching him and he nodded pleasantly at her, all the while wanting to knock in her snooty face and show her who was boss. He let his eyes wander over the store casually, seeing no one else except his pigeon and the woman's red-haired partner, who looked like a Republican lawyer on the make. Good. Piece of cake.

The blond guy produced the pint and Burnett paid for it. "Thanks,'' he told the cashier, then nodded to the bitch. "Ma'am.''

He walked out the door, prepared to disperse his troops to firefight positions. Instead he barely got outside before seeing Cleavon approaching, with

Coolie arguing with him and Juke trailing behind. They were all carrying shotguns.

"What the hell are you doing?" he demanded, grabbing the long-haired man's arm.

Cleavon jerked his arm away and glared at Burnett. "I'm just gonna go take care of this shit, that's all," he announced. "I'm sick of your big-deal military crap."

"You stupid son of—"

Cleavon pushed him aside. "See you in hell, sucker," he said as he strode through the door.

"Back him up!" Burnett yelled, ripping the .45 from the waistband of his pants, charging the door.

He had it halfway open when Cleavon's first shot exploded through the plywood counter, throwing the blond kid backward, screaming. Then everything seemed to happen in flashes. Burnett got through the door. Cleavon pumped his second shot. The woman's hand came out of her purse with a .45. She blasted the punk in the belly from a distance of five feet.

Cleavon spun then crashed to the floor, giving Burnett a clear shot at the woman. For a second she stared with wide eyes at the man she had shot. That hesitation let Burnett's first shot catch her in mid-thigh. She fell, firing wildly at him as he dived away into one of the narrow aisles. The woman seized her chance to crawl to cover behind a display of single bottles of wine cooler, chilling in a barrel full of ice. The screams of the youth behind the counter were punctuated by Cleavon's guttural curses.

Then Coolie and Juke were through the door, charging into the guts of the place. Burnett jumped gleefully to his feet, firing through a line of wine bottles at the bodyguard in the far corner. Bottles exploded in succession, crashing all around him. The red-haired man ducked, bottles broke and liquor poured all over the store, the floors becoming slick, and strewn with shards of shattered glass.

"Concentrate fire!" Burnett yelled. Juke and Coolie were in the aisles, shooting randomly at the corner. Remembering the bitch, Burnett turned to the barrel of wine cooler at the front of the store, firing at an exposed section of the woman's leg, hitting her in a hail of glass and wine. She crawled around the other side of the barrel and returned fire, driving him farther into the store.

He saw movement in the aisle beside him and came over the top of the shelves. His pigeon was on hands and knees, trying to crawl to safety.

"Hey, buddy," he called. As the man looked up, Burnett extended his arm over the racks and squeezed off a shot. The old man's head disintegrated into a shower of blood and brains.

In the back of the store Juke and Coolie had dumped over a whole aisle of racks. The bodyguard went down in a pile of broken glass. Burnett rushed to add his fire to the others', tearing the already dead body to pieces.

"Now what?" Coolie's jaw was clenched, his breath coming fast.

Burnett looked around. "Did you ever wonder what a fire in a place like this would be like?"

"What about the woman?" Coolie asked.

"She's down and cornered," Burnett said. "Let's do it."

They ran back through the store, coming up the aisle that Cleavon had dragged himself into. He was sitting in a puddle of blood and liquor.

"Shit! The bitch blew out my stomach!" he yelled. "Get me outta this damn place!"

"Can you walk?" Burnett asked.

"If I could walk, asshole, do you think I'd be laying here?"

Juke bent down to pick him up.

"Wait!" Burnett grinned. "Looks like a belly wound, my friend. Ain't nothin' we can do about no belly wound."

"Get me to a goddamn hospital!" Cleavon yelled.

"We gotta hurry," Coolie said. "We've been here too long."

"C'mon, Burnett!" Cleavon yelled, pulling his hand away to look at the gaping wound in his abdomen. "This shit is gonna kill me if you don't."

The man's gun lay beside him on the floor. Burnett gently pushed it out of reach with his foot. "I think you're already dead, partner," he said, laughing and stepping over the wounded man's legs. "Let's go, people!"

"Burnett!" Cleavon screamed. "I'll kill you!"

Burnett turned and snapped off a crisp salute. "Take your best shot, partner."

They hurried past the counter, the screaming boy just moaning now as the life drained out of him. A steady stream of blood was flowing out from under the wine display.

"Outside," Burnett ordered. "Quick. Coolie, start the car."

Coolie and Juke ran outside, while Burnett took a disposable lighter from a display near the counter. "Whoever's still alive in here," he called, "you're in for a hot time!"

He laughed, enjoying power in a way he had thought he'd never exercise again. God, this was as much fun as Nam! He'd torched many villages there.

He picked up a late-edition newspaper from a rack near the door, checking the late sports scores as the Cadillac pulled around in front, Coolie behind the wheel motioning him to hurry.

Backing out the door, he fired the disposable lighter, touching it to the rolled-up paper. Coolie had leaned over and opened the passenger door for him. As the flame climbed the paper, he tossed it into the store and jumped in the car.

The fire spread rapidly across the floor of the building, a pure blue-and-white alcohol flame, far prettier than the orange gas and napalm fires in Vietnam.

"Pull around the side again," he ordered.

"We gotta get out of here," Coolie objected.

"Just do like I say!" Burnett ejected the clip from the butt of the .45, picking a fresh one from the seat and stuffing it in with a click.

Coolie backed up, tires squealing, and came around the side of the building where the picture window gave them an excellent view of the inside. Burnett rolled down the window.

Fire had spread through the entire structure, fueled by hundreds of bottles of spilled liquor. Near the front, where the flames were the highest, bottles began exploding in bright white balls of flame. It was the most beautiful thing Burnett had ever seen.

They had a perfect view of the woman. Flames all around her, she nevertheless had managed to dismantle the wine cooler display, pulling two long metal poles from it. Using one of them as a crutch, she pulled herself with difficulty to her feet. With whatever strength, she began swinging the other pole, banging it against the plate-glass window.

"I hear sirens!" Coolie yelled. "We gotta..."

"In a minute." Burnett smiled at the woman's efforts to free herself.

All at once the window cracked, then shattered into thousands of pieces. The rush of smoke and heat pouring through the opening could be felt in the car.

As the woman used the pole to knock out the remaining pieces of glass, Burnett took the safety off the gun and snapped one into the chamber.

Hair singed, she was just trying to climb through the opening when Burnett sighted down at her good leg and squeezed one off, shattering her knee in bloody fragments. Her face twisted in pain and she was knocked back into the inferno.

"Okay," he said, smiling at the others. "Let's get the hell out of here."

Coolie peeled out, just seconds before a fire engine came roaring down the street, passing them.

Burnett turned in the seat and watched out the back window as the building rumbled on its foundation with the force of hundreds of small explosions. Finally the walls collapsed inward as a brilliant ball of white light rose majestically in the sky, lighting the night like a man-made sunrise. The man realized then that above all he was an artist, rendering his own form of destructive magic on an unappreciative world.

7

It was almost midnight. Bolan, Carver and even the Giancarlos had spent the evening securing the windows and doors on the first floor of the big house. Now Bolan sat in the kitchen staring at a plate of spaghetti, for which he had no appetite at all. It wasn't that he wasn't hungry, he just couldn't seem to bring himself to eat food that might have been purchased at the expense of someone's life. Perhaps that made him an idealist.

Carver sat across from him, drinking a cup of coffee that he had brought back from a convenience store. He hadn't even pretended to try to eat here.

"You know," he said, "I grew up in a dead end neighborhood where nobody seemed to have a chance in life. I wanted to believe that America wasn't like that, that a man could make a good life for himself, no matter who he was. I worked to put myself through college, then went to work for the Company so I could try to defend the ideals I wanted to believe in, all over the world. You know what I ended up doing?" He shook his head and took another sip. "They were training me to teach Central American peasants to write anti-American slogans on walls so that the ruling juntas could launch antiterrorist campaigns and ask the American Congress for more money to fight the terrorists that I was inventing. It was stupid."

"The Company's too political," Bolan said, stating the obvious.

"So I quit that and end up here, laying my life on the line for some cheap hood who calls me a jungle bunny and makes me sleep in his kitchen." Carver set the cup down hard on the table. "What's it all mean?"

"I don't know, Roy." Bolan pushed his plate aside. "I don't like what goes on any more than you do. The bureaucracy doesn't exist to serve the people anymore, it exists to serve itself."

Carver sighed and sat back in his chair, looking around the large, modern kitchen. "Seems they should be here by now if they're coming."

"Yeah?" Bolan shook his head. "Actually, I think this will be the last place hit."

"Why do you say that?"

"Because it should have been hit first."

"What do we do tonight?"

"We'll take four-hour watches," Bolan replied. "Go out and check around right now, then get some rest. I'll take the first watch."

"Sounds like a deal," Carver said, standing, "though I don't know if I can sleep on that son of a bitch's bed or not."

Bolan gave a tired smile and a wave as Carver left.

He felt absolutely no sense of danger or urgency, which bothered him more than if he did, because it meant that one of his other teams was coming under the gun tonight. He was worried about their lack of training and experience, remembering how easily Joey Giancarlo had gotten the drop on them. And he was afraid because they were good people, and good people rarely seemed to stay alive for long around Bolan.

The door to the dining room swung open, Angela Giancarlo coming through with an armful of dishes—there was nothing wrong with the Giancarlos' appetites.

The woman carried the plates to the sink and set them down loudly. Then she noticed his full plate.

"What's wrong?" she asked. "Don't you like my cooking?"

"You'd better be thinking about getting back to your hotel," he said. "I really don't want you around for this."

She sat down across from him in the chair that Carver had vacated. "Why do you dislike my family so much?" she asked.

"You're a big girl. You figure it out."

"I haven't done anything to you."

"I know you haven't."

She looked at him sadly. "I know my father hasn't led the best of lives. I'm not that naive. But when I look around at all the corruption, not just in criminal circles but in politics, in government, I don't see that what Old Sam does is that much different, or any worse."

"You're talking to the wrong man, lady," Bolan stated with conviction. "What you're saying, basically, is that because some people behave like animals it's all right for other people to behave like animals. Sorry. I don't buy it.''

"How about you? I'll bet you're not lily-white, either. I mean, give the old man a break. He's out of all that now, he's retired. Joey's even running a string of legitimate businesses for him."

"You don't retire on the blood of innocent people," Bolan said harshly. "And I've heard about his 'legitimate businesses'—Lucky Sam's Body Shops. He used to have body shops in Chicago, too, except they were called chop shops, where stolen cars were altered and painted for resale."

"That was a long time ago."

"Right," Bolan said. "I was reading the *Oklahoma City Times* this afternoon and it's interesting that auto thefts in the area have increased by fifty percent."

Her eyes flashed angrily. "You son of a bitch."

"Look," he replied. "I'm not blaming you. You didn't ask to have a mafioso for a father. So maybe the string ends with you. It happens."

She shrugged.

Bolan decided to give the woman a break and change the subject. "I heard your father say earlier that you're a writer."

"I guess you can say that," she said. "I've had my name on the credit line of a lot of movies, anyway."

"Such modesty," he said.

"It's not modesty, Mr. Belasko—"

"Mike."

She smiled, a warm smile. "Mike. It's just that I've noticed that every film I've ever worked on ultimately has Giancarlo money behind it somehow, and that every script I've ever written is rewritten when I'm done with it, to the point that none of *my* work remains." She looked down at the tabletop, embarrassed. "I guess you could say that my father's bought me a pretty good career."

"I'm sorry," Bolan said sincerely. "Maybe you should refuse the help and try it on your own."

"I'm afraid I'm not that strong," she replied, "and not that good."

He reached across the table and took her hands in his. "Trust yourself. I'll bet you're better than you think."

She took his hand and lightly brushed it against her cheek. "That may be the nicest thing anyone's ever said to me."

"Then I really do feel for you."

"Angie!" Old Sam called from the dining room. "Where you at, girl? Come on in here!"

She dropped Bolan's hand and stood. "His master's voice. I'd better see what's up."

He watched her walk to the door, wondering if he was being foolish to feel sorry for her. "Get out of here soon," he reminded her.

Halfway through the door she turned back to him. "You're really concerned about my safety, aren't you?"

"Don't look so surprised," he replied. "And when you're ready to leave, have me or Roy go out to the car with you, just to check."

"Okay," she said, smiling warmly. The door swung closed behind her.

A few minutes later the back door opened and Roy Carver stepped back in. "It's like a morgue out there," he announced. "The whole damn neighborhood's a ghost town."

Bolan picked up his plate and walked to the sink. "It's not going to happen here tonight," he said. "I just know it. I should be with the others." He heard a distant phone ringing, its sound triggered his heightened senses.

"You can't do everything," Carver told him. "Giancarlo seems like the logical candidate for prime target. It only makes sense for you to be here."

"Yeah," Bolan returned. "But a lot of things about this deal defy logic."

The door swung open, Joey Giancarlo poking his head into the kitchen. "You gotta phone call," he said and held out an unplugged phone.

Bolan took it from him. "Where do I..."

"The jack's in the wall." Joey's face looked strained. As Bolan walked to plug in the phone and set it on the counter, Giancarlo said, "You stay away from my sister."

"Your sister's all grown up now," Bolan returned. "She can pick her own friends."

"Not you, she can't." The man pointed a finger. "Just stay away from her."

Bolan turned his back to Joey and lifted the receiver. "Belasko," he said, his warrior's senses tuned up high.

"Striker... it's me, Hal." Brognola's voice was strained.

"What's wrong?"

"They hit Stinky Barberi a little while ago."

"What about our people?" Bolan asked.

"They're still sorting through things.... It's quite a mess."

"Our people," Bolan repeated.

"It's confusion here, Striker," the Fed explained. "It happened at a liquor store, and there was a fire. But preliminaries indicate that Barberi, Lomax, a counter man, plus one of the shooters were killed."

"What about Carol Niven?"

"She's really bad," he said, his voice shaky. "She was shot several times and left for dead in the fire, and she's burned over ninety percent of her body. They've already got her in surgery to amputate her left leg."

"Damn," Bolan whispered. "Damn."

"What is it?" Carver asked. Bolan waved him off.

"Anything else?" Bolan asked.

"Our man on the phone taps picked up something tonight that may prove useful."

"Our leak?"

"Yeah. They're on their way to pick him up now."

"Keep me posted, Hal," Bolan said, "and charter me a plane. I'm going to Seattle."

"But we really need you on Giancarlo," Brognola protested. "He's the important—"

"No," Bolan cut in impatiently. "They're saving him for some reason. He won't come under the gun until Ottoni's out of the way."

"Striker, I—"

"Don't say it, Hal. You told me I could do it my way. My way is to go and see Carol Niven, then head for Denver where Joan is next in line. What about the dead punk?"

"They're rushing through ID now, though he was burned so badly..."

"Let me know what you find out." Bolan looked at his watch. "I'm taking Carver with me. Get that plane ready, I'm only fifteen minutes from the airport."

Even over the long distance lines he heard Brognola's loud sigh. "I hope you know what you're doing."

"I'm setting things straight."

Bolan hung up the phone. Then he looked at Carver.

"It's Lomax, isn't it?" Carver asked.

Bolan nodded silently.

Carver's hard face softened, his eyes misting over. "Oh, man, not like that," he said. "Jesus. Neal was only twenty-four years old."

Joey Giancarlo was still standing in the doorway, shaking his head. "Some bodyguards you guys turn out to be," he said. "I'd have been better off hiring a bunch of neighborhood kids."

Bolan turned to the man, his rage a cold fire within him. Without thought, he reached out and grabbed

Joey by the front of his shirt, hauled him through the doorway, then cocked a big right hand.

"Touch me and you're dead!" Giancarlo growled.

"The hell I am," Bolan replied, and took him hard to the mouth. He fell across the table, sending food and dishes crashing to the floor. With a heavy thud, he hit the linoleum.

"Thanks," Roy Carver said. "I needed that."

KEN CHASEN SAT ON THE BED in the dark, his eyes all but glued open, his brain spinning like a pinwheel. The open plastic bag of coke lay beside him, the straw poking out of it so he could easily dip down and take a snort whenever he had the urge—and he had the urge constantly.

The only light in the room came from the screen of the television set. For the eighth time he played the tape of him and Yvette, marveling at the woman—her beauty, her passion—and his own responses.

The luminous numbers of his bedside clock told him it was 3:00 a.m., at least they did when he could summon the concentration to focus his eyes on the numbers. Day or night were all the same to him now.

The phone had rung many times since Marie had taken the kids away, but he wouldn't answer it. He'd show her. He didn't need her sniveling, whiny ways. She could stay away and rot for all he cared. What did she know of what his life was like? How could she understand the pressures he had to endure from assholes like that son of a bitch Kaminsky, with his beady little eyes and his tiny soft hands and his conniving brain. Well, he didn't need any of them now. Yvette would look out for him.

He watched her on the TV, magnetized by her beautiful body and her animal nature. She charged him up, made him greater than himself. That was real love there on the screen, enduring passion beyond anything ordinary people could ever comprehend. He leaned down and snorted out of the open bag.

Suddenly he heard a noise outside. He got off the bed quietly and went to peek out the window. There were three cars in his driveway, one of them a Virginia police cruiser. Cops?

His first thought was that Marie had turned him in. Then he saw the little shit climbing out of one of the cars—Kaminsky. The man had figured him out.

He looked around the room frantically. They couldn't take him. He was only a day away from meeting with Yvette. He just needed to stay free long enough to reach her. What to do? What to do?

Clothes were his first thought. All he was wearing was a pair of jeans. Had to hurry. Hurry. He sat on the bed, nearly knocking over the bag of coke in his haste, and struggled into tennis shoes, his hands shaking. Hurry. A wrinkled T-shirt lay on the bed. No time. He grabbed it and wrapped it around the cocaine bag, then ran back to the window.

There were six of them walking toward the front of the house, the police in the lead. That probably meant a warrant. *God, an arrest warrant!* He couldn't let them take him. He had to get to Yvette. She'd save him. She would fix everything.

He rushed through the bedroom, charging down the dark, shadowy hall that seemed to stretch out to infinity before him. The floor seemed tilted, uneven, his house an alien landscape. He reached the top of the stairs and tripped, falling, the stairs rushing up to meet him, then helping him down. He bounced three, four times, then hit the floor hard and jumped right up, feeling no pain at all.

Hurry.

He ran to the back door. His fingers felt thick and useless as he fumbled with the lock. He could hear the front doorbell as he tore open the door, and the polite gesture struck him as funny. He ran out into the large backyard, his mongrel dog Skipper playfully running up and nipping at his legs.

Now what? He could hear their voices. They'd come around to the back door any moment. A six-foot security fence enclosed his backyard. Most of the neighbors kept large dogs to keep out the increasing number of intruders here in the suburbs. Where to go?

The dog jumped at him again and he pushed it away, looking around frantically, not even noticing the near freezing air as he ran around without a shirt. There was nothing in back except Skipper's doghouse. He looked at it. It had a hinge on its floor that allowed the entire house section to be raised for cleaning. Sure. Sure.

HAL BROGNOLA STOOD out on the front lawn of the Chasen house, watching the policemen at the door unsuccessfully trying to gain entry. It was late. He was tired. There'd already been killing tonight. It took something out of him that didn't spring back as it used to.

Two of his men stood chatting quietly and smoking cigarettes as they leaned against Chasen's Corvette. "You guys go and check around the back," he said, then looked at the attorney general's liaison. "Where would he go? Any ideas?"

"I have no idea," Kaminsky said. "Mr. Brognola, this whole thing is a shock to me. I've known Ken for ten years, ever since he hired on at Justice. He's the last person I would ever have suspected of anything like this. Then there was your wiretap, and the call from Marie. The way she sounded, he could be anywhere."

One of the cops walked up to report. "I don't think he's in there."

"We have to know for sure, Sergeant," Brognola said. "Break in. That's what the warrant's for."

"Yes, sir."

The man hurried off to his cruiser, coming back with a large crowbar and heading to the door.

"Where did he hang out when he wasn't working?" Hal asked Kaminsky. "What did he like to do?"

"He was...is, a workaholic," Kaminsky said. "Three times a week we played racquetball in the basement gym, and the other nights we'd stop by for a drink at Phillips. That was it as far as I know."

Brognola looked at the man. As far as he knew— what a line. Here was a top Justice Department lawyer who had compromised the security of the United

States and run thick and fast with organized crime, and nobody knows anything.

There was a rending of wood as the door cracked and splintered under the relentless drive of the crowbar. When it gave with a final loud creak, the police rushed in with drawn weapons.

"I'm going to go look around back," Brognola said, walking off. Kaminsky went with him.

"What will happen to Ken?" he asked as Brognola reached the already open gate, a small dog running out as he and Kaminsky walked in.

"You tell me, Counselor," Brognola replied. "Our federal statutes provide pretty stiff criminal penalties for the kind of conspiracy Chasen's been involved with, but they never seem to hold up once you guys get in there plea-bargaining and making compromises."

"Was the wiretap legal?" Kaminsky returned.

"I'll take the Fifth on that one."

"Well, that answers my question," Kaminsky said as they wandered into a large, well-kept backyard with edged walkways, gardens with a few fall flowers, a doghouse and a brick barbecue grill. "It's true that if he was willing to turn on his sources, given the illegal nature of those sources, well . . ."

"Don't tell me," Brognola said. "He could end up as a protected witness himself."

"I'd probably suggest that very thing," Kaminsky acknowledged.

CHASEN SAT CRAMPED UP in the doghouse, the smell all but overpowering, his limbs sore and aching. He'd heard several people's voices in the backyard, one of them Kaminsky's. But unfortunately, due to the nature of his hideout, he couldn't hear what was being said.

He hated them, hated them all. He wished he could just jump out of the doghouse and take on them all, but he held himself back. Later. There'd be other chances. And besides, there were different, more powerful urges to deal with at the moment.

Unfolding his T-shirt, he quietly eased the plastic bag out of it, gently cradling the white powder like a baby.

8

Bolan hated hospitals, especially late at night when the lights were turned down and white-clad women with silent shoes glided wraithlike through antiseptic corridors, making the place seem like a huge mausoleum. He and Carver walked down the hall of the fifth floor intensive care unit, both silent as they tried to deal with their losses in their own way. Bolan hadn't known Lomax or petite, conscientious Carol Niven very well, but he had liked them. They'd been willing to give of themselves unselfishly and without question, which was far more than he could say for the people they'd been protecting.

The outcome was a tragedy to Bolan, as was every wasted life.

He didn't need to look at the room numbers to find his way, but just headed toward the big state trooper who stood guard at the end of the hall. The man's face was somber but alert as he moved up to address him.

"My name's Belasko," Bolan said.

"We had a call about you from the Justice Department." The trooper, a lieutenant, sized him up. "They brought her down from surgery about thirty minutes ago."

"How does it look?" Bolan asked.

The man shook his head and looked at the floor.

"Can we go in?"

The trooper nodded. "Fine by me, but the doctors might have other ideas." He stepped away from the door, pushing it open for Bolan and Carver.

They walked in. Carver gave a strangled groan as they approached the bed. She was swathed in bandages, the sheets oddly flat where the leg that had been taken off should have been. Four IV lines were dripping blood and clear fluids into her body, while tubes in her nose and mouth helped her breathe and keep her chest clear.

A white-coated doctor was bent over her, checking vital signs and writing on a chart. He had heard Carver's exclamation, and walked over to them, his face set angrily.

"Would you please leave," he said in an exaggerated whisper. "My patient can have no visitors."

"Is she conscious?" Bolan pulled identification out of his wallet and showed it to the man.

"In and out," the doctor told him, turning to look at her. "But she can't talk."

"How is she?" Carver seemed unable to take his eyes from her.

The man lowered his voice even more. "If she lives through the night it will be a miracle. Now please..." He tried to usher them toward the door.

"If she's conscious I must try to speak with her," Bolan said.

"No. Absolutely not. She's been through enough."

"Other lives depend on it," Bolan returned. "No disrespect intended..."

"D-doctor..." Niven rasped weakly from the bed. "Please..."

The man tightened his jaw and moved to the woman, putting his ear near her mouth. In a moment he returned to Bolan and Carver. "Please keep it as brief as you can," he said. "Every bit of strength she uses to talk takes away from what she needs to live."

"I understand," Bolan said, moving past the doctor to stand before Niven. Her face was slack and expressionless, already given over to death. He'd seen that goodbye look many times and found himself saying his own silent farewells to her even as he watched.

He bent down close to her. "I'm so sorry," he said.

"I b-blew it," she rasped. "But I g-got...one of them."

"You did just fine," Bolan said softly. He heard Carver sob beside him, tears running freely down his face.

"I know this will be hard for you," Bolan said, "but you must try to help me a little so I can get the people who did this to you. Do you remember anything at all?"

"Not after the sh-shooting started," she whispered. "I just remember...pain. But before... before..." She closed her eyes for several seconds, biting her lower lip. She took some shallow breaths and opened her eyes. The hair was singed completely from her brows and lashes. "They came in a w-white Cadillac. I remember...saw it at B-Barberi's house, but didn't think...think..."

"Never mind that." Bolan turned to Carver. "Take notes."

He nodded, his face strained with sadness as he reached into his sport jacket for the pad and pen.

Bolan turned back to the dying woman. "How many?" he asked.

"F-four. With sh-shotguns."

"Now this is very important, Carol," he said. "Think carefully before you answer."

She nodded silently.

"Okay. What were the men like? How were they dressed?"

"P-punks," she said. "Trashed Army...fatigues. They en-enjoyed it. God, they—"

The woman's eyes widened in remembered horror, her body coming up off the bed despite her injuries.

The doctor rushed back over, saying, "I told you not to do this."

"We're nearly finished, Doctor," Bolan told him.

"No, that's it."

"Doctor...please," Niven said as the doctor eased her back to a reclining position. Every movement was obviously agonizing.

The doctor backed away, glaring at both men.

"Your description didn't sound like Mafia hoods," he said.

"N-no," she whispered. "Not...Mafia. More like...like mercenaries."

Bolan looked at Carver, who raised his eyebrows in confusion as he wrote, then Bolan turned back to Niven. "Can you remember anything else?"

"Long...braided hair," she whispered. "And one of them...them..." Her eyes widened in fear. "Burnett...they c-called him...Burnett." She was breathing rapidly now, excitedly, her bandaged hands shaking in front of her. "Get him...oh, God...he's...insane! Please...get him...please. Please!"

The doctor was there at once. "That's it!" he snapped. "No more. Leave now." He turned to tend to the woman, small moans and cries escaping from her trembling lips.

"Mike..." Carver said.

Bolan took him by the arm instead and led him out of the room into the hallway. Carver was shaking, his lips pulled tight.

"I'm gonna kill those sons of bitches," he said low, his hands balled into fists. "I'll tear them apart with my bare hands if I have to, but so help me God—"

"No!" Bolan said firmly. "We'll get them. We'll get them in Denver. But not that way."

"You saw...you saw..." the man told him.

"Listen to me," Bolan said. "All you ever get with hot blood is a slab in the morgue. We'll get them because it's our job, and because they're mad dogs who have to be taken off the streets. But we'll do it cold and in control. There'll be time to mourn when this is all over."

"You must be made of ice," Carver accused him angrily.

"No, Roy," Bolan said, hardening himself to his own memories. "I'm not made of ice. I'm just selfish. I don't want to lose any more friends."

BENITO VILLANI SAT PATIENTLY in the back seat of his black limo, parked on Jefferson Street in Joliet, Illinois. Through its dark-tinted windows he watched the sunrise. Patience, he mused, is the virtue of the old, who finally realize, at the point where ailments and pains don't go away, that all people are waiting patiently for death. Despite what Mother Church had told him all his life, he knew immortality was achieved not through death, but through children who carry on the family name—an investment in the future that Old Sam Giancarlo had tried to take away from him. Instead he would take it away from Old Sam Giancarlo.

Vic D'matto turned around in the front seat to look at him. "Can I get you some coffee, Mr. Villani?" he asked.

The old man shook his head. "Thank you, no, Vic," he replied, taking for granted D'matto's loyalty, and that of his brother-in-law Tony who sat beside him up front. They were just soldiers, owing their allegiance to him. Another thing age had taught Villani was that everyone serves some master, and that the reward comes through the service itself. People crave direction.

He and Giancarlo had been sworn enemies for more than fifty years, and he couldn't remember a time when either of them wasn't preoccupied with plotting the destruction of the other. Now, as they aged, their war seemed to have moved to a metaphysical plane— they were fighting for their very souls, using the lives of their children as the bargaining chits. Giancarlo's betrayal of all the ideals of *cosa nostra* was merely his grand gesture in the battle for the hereafter, his subsequent "retirement" being his claim of success. But it wasn't over, not yet. Though two of Villani's sons lay dead, Rocco still lived to carry out the blood oath of revenge.

"I think they're comin'," Tony Ferrari said. Villani sat up a little straighter to look down the all-but-deserted roadway five miles from the prison.

He heard the heavy rumble first, then seconds later the lumbering garage truck came into view in the distance. "Get ready for them," he said quietly, and D'matto and Ferrari obediently climbed out of the car, moving to the front of it.

The garbage truck drove toward them, its grinding sound signifying the end of pastoral morning and the coming of the human beasts to the quiet world. The truck rumbled closer, whining and rattling to a stop close to the limousine.

Two men in filthy overalls jumped out of the truck and ran around to its rear. They were Villani's people; he ran the Illinois garbage racket. A minute later they reappeared lugging a large, gray plastic garbage can between them. After setting it down, they slit the black plastic garbage bag inside the can with a small knife. Rocco climbed out of the confining container and took a deep breath, then raised his fists in triumph. Vic paid off the garbage collectors and sent them on their way.

Rocco grinned broadly as he hurried around to the limousine's back door, pulling it open. "Hey, Pop!" he cried, climbing into the car. A rush of smelly air entered with him and Ben pulled out a handkerchief and put it to his nose.

"You smell rotten," he commented.

"Yeah, gross huh?" Rocco removed two cotton wads from his nose. "Thought I'd go nuts in there for a while. Man, am I glad to see you!"

Villani eyed his son carefully. "You look healthy and well fed."

"Yeah, sure," Rocco said. "They looked out for me in there. They knew whose boy I was."

D'matto and Ferrari had climbed back in the limo, and D'matto started it up.

"How long before they miss you?" Villani asked.

"Not for a couple hours yet." Rocco looked out the window at the scenery sliding past. "Where are we going?"

"Not far," the old man answered. "Joliet District airport." He reached down to the floor and pulled up a small suitcase, handing it to Rocco. "Here, put these on."

Rocco stripped off his prison shirt, opening the power window to throw it out, and pulled a dress shirt out of the suitcase. "How come you waited so long to spring me, Pop?" he asked as he buttoned the pale blue shirt.

"I didn't have a good enough reason," Villani replied, reaching into the suitcase to pick out a tie that matched the shirt. He handed it to Rocco. "And I hoped I could fix it some other way."

"You couldn't?"

The old man shook his head, watching Rocco trying to wriggle out of his prison jeans, almost wishing that it had been Rocco who died instead of his brothers. They were so much smarter, so much better managers. "There's too many indictments comin' down," he said. "I couldn't make no headway."

Rocco threw the jeans out the window and reversed his comical gyrations while trying to get into a pair of dress pants. "But I heard you were takin' care of Giancarlo and his people."

"His people," Ben said, "but not him. I've saved him for you."

Rocco's eyes lit up as he began to fumble with his tie. "You're gonna let me kill Old Sam?"

"Yeah," Villani said. "You gonna kill Old Sam and that son of his, Joey, too."

"All right!" Rocco cheered, then leaned toward the front seat. "You hear that, Vic?"

"Yeah, I heard," Vic said. "We're goin' with you, me and Tony."

Rocco's face darkened and he sat back. Ben shook his head as he watched realization sink in. "But, Pop," Rocco asked, "how'd you figure out where they were hidin'?"

"Don't you worry about that," Villani told him. "What you gotta worry about is what the hell you're gonna do when the job's done. Now straighten your tie, it's crooked."

"Just like the rest of me, huh?" Rocco grinned, pulling in his chin to look down at the tie. "Okay, what *am* I gonna do after?"

"Once we kill Old Sam," Villani said, "I figure we'll send you away for a while... maybe to Rio, who knows? Then, with the Giancarlos out of the way, the government ain't got no witnesses or no indictments. We're back in business good, then. That's when I start the wheels turnin' to get the charges against you thrown out and get you back home."

"Rio sounds good. I hear the broads are real sweet on American boys."

"You leave them foreign broads alone," Villani warned. "They just give you diseases."

"Pop, any broad sounds good to me right now."

The old man waved off the suggestion. "Broads is all you ever think about. Wait till things settle down, son, then we'll find you a nice Italian Catholic girl, like your mama. Right now you got business to think about."

"Here we are," Vic called to them as they approached a small municipal airport for private and charter planes. He drove the limo toward a Lear jet out on the flight line as Rocco slipped into the suit coat that went with the pants.

"How do I look, Pop?" he asked.

"Like a gorilla in a suit," Villani said with a smile. The car pulled to a stop by the jet, and stairs were immediately lowered from its cabin.

As Rocco closed the suitcase, Ben fished around in his pocket, coming out with a piece of paper, which he handed to his son. "Here's the address, and the address of somebody down there who'll get you some hardware."

Rocco opened the door. "Oklahoma City?" he said, incredulous, as he got out.

"I want you to do it tomorrow night."

Rocco leaned back in through the car door. "Why not tonight? We'll already be down—"

"I got my reasons, okay?" Villani replied. "And, Rocco..."

"Yeah, Pop?"

"Make sure you do Joey right. I want you to put the gun to his head and do him yourself."

Rocco nodded solemnly. "The vendetta ends here, my father. I pledge my life to that."

"Good boy," Villani said, nodding. "Good boy."

9

The ever-present pollution hung low that morning, thanks to a high-pressure area that had made its way over the Rockies and was hanging over Denver's large industrial belt. The mile-high cityscape had become wide open country as Bolan and Carver closed on Ottoni's lakefront property, the Air Force jeep he had requisitioned at Lowry Air Base coming in handy on the rugged terrain. Somehow it seemed fitting that Ottoni should live here on his government paycheck, where more people, per capita, worked for the state and federal governments than anywhere else in the country.

The jeep had no top. Bolan found the frigid air cleansing and refreshing after a sleepless night, the visit to the dying Carol Niven in a Seattle hospital, and hours of traveling. It reminded him that being alive was a good thing. Roy Carver didn't seem to feel the same way.

"God, it's cold!" the man said, hugging himself. "Why did I let you talk me into this?"

"You didn't," Bolan returned. "I made you."

Bolan loved Colorado, a Spanish word meaning "red," named after the Rio Grande. He had an affinity for its wide open, rugged freedom and unequaled beauty. If he ever retired and settled down, it would be here. If he lived that long.

Bolan geared down to second as Bear Creek Canyon Road ascended steeply. The countryside stretched out around them, browns and purples dominating the landscape, all of it forming a background for the magnificence of Mount Evans, which towered nearly fifteen thousand feet high.

They crested the hill. Less than a mile away Big Bear Lake and the expensive houses around it came into view. Ottoni was a lawyer, and apparently a successful one. He had been Old Sam's *consigliere* for a good many years, handling family business along with his own criminal practice. The work had apparently paid off, for the exclusive community right on the lake was obviously one only the very wealthy could afford.

Bolan saw at once why Ottoni had opted for staying here instead of taking to the *mattresses*. The entire neighborhood was surrounded by a high brick wall with only one guarded entrance. He pulled up to the guardhouse beside the automatic gate, where a middle-aged man in a uniform was coming out and looking over him and his jeep.

The man examined Bolan's identification, then went back in the guardhouse and raised the barrier. Bolan pulled up closer to the gate, and asked, "Is there someone on duty all night?"

"Yes, sir," the guard answered.

"Tell him to keep his eyes open tonight," Bolan said, and drove into the small, exclusive development.

Ottoni's house was only a block from the gate, a huge boxy structure that looked more like a penitentiary than a home. Perhaps Ottoni's former life had influenced his taste in architecture. His property was surrounded by a six-foot wall with a security gate. The man certainly believed in protection.

Bolan hit the horn. In a minute Benny Young poked his head out the front then, recognizing Bolan, he went inside to release the gate lock. Seconds later the gate swung open. By the time Bolan had parked the jeep behind several other cars in the driveway at the back, Young and Joan Meredith were hurrying out the back door to greet him. They were followed, slowly, by an older man, who must once have been thickset and muscular but was now gone to fat—Ottoni.

Meredith, strain showing in her face, moved right up and into Bolan's arms, hugging him quickly then pulling away. "I just got a call from Seattle," she said, tears welling up in her eyes. "Carol died a few minutes ago."

Bolan nodded and looked at Carver, both men knowing that it was for the best. "They'll hit here next," he said. "This time we'll be ready for them."

Ottoni walked up to Bolan and gave him the once-over. Bolan returned his stare. The Mafia lawyer had small, narrow eyes and large jowls, his mouth set in a permanent frown. His silk suit had wide lapels and he wore about three pounds of gold jewelry. "So you're the big deal from the Justice Department,'' he drawled. ''I want to register a complaint. When I signed on for this bargain, I was promised protection. Four lousy plainclothes agents aren't going to keep out Villani's people if they know where I am.''

''They why didn't you let us move you?'' Bolan asked.

''I got a business here with people who don't know who I am. I got a life here. I got a house with every security device available.'' He pointed a stubby finger at Bolan's face. ''The deal was, you creeps would protect me—not move me, not hide me—protect me. Protect me where I stand, where I live.''

''So that's what we intend to do,'' Bolan said.

''Not with four lousy agents!'' The man waved a hand at Benny Young. ''Hell, this one's so green he needs someone to wipe his nose. How are people like this going to protect me?''

''You wouldn't let us ask for any help from the local authorities,'' Meredith reminded him.

''Of course I wouldn't,'' the man replied. ''All I need is for the local cops to know who I am. They'd have me run out of here in two weeks. *You* people are supposed to protect me, not anybody else.''

''The Justice Department feels that four agents for one man are sufficient,'' Bolan said firmly, holding the man's eyes with his own. Then he shrugged. ''You don't want us, we'll go. You want to complain, do it to someone who gives a damn. And I'll tell you something else, I'm not your boy to shove around or give orders to. Don't get in my way.''

The man backed up a step. The fear edging over his face explained everything to Bolan. The man was a coward, used to intimidating people in social settings, but unaccustomed to confrontations where people tried to intimidate him. He had lived soft, on the periphery of criminal circles, never learning how to survive on the street. He was pushing so hard because he was scared to death.

"No need to get touchy," Ottoni said quietly. He turned and walked back toward the house. Bolan was satisfied that the emotional hell Ottoni was living in right now was more than adequate compensation for the harm he had done in the past.

Carver retrieved their overnight bags from the back of the jeep, while Bolan looked around to take stock of the house and grounds in relation to the lake. The water was calm, reflecting the beauty of the mountains around it. It also might provide a measure of protection from the rear. From what he'd seen of their antagonists, they weren't clever enough to consider the subtlety of approaching from the back. It made defenses much easier.

The backyard was small. A cement patio with grill was bordered by a small area of grass. The main feature at the back of the property was the small pier and speedboat tied up there. As they walked to the house, Joan Meredith moved up next to Bolan.

"It's a hell of a deal," she said. "I hear it was pretty rough up in Seattle."

"They're animals," the Executioner replied, "but they're not very smart. If we don't blow it somehow, I think we can take them tonight."

"You sure they're coming?" she asked as they reached the sliding patio door and moved into the spacious kitchen.

"Positive, but I couldn't tell you why. For some reason, they're saving Old Sam for last."

"They're not Mafia, are they?"

Bolan shook his head. "Let's get into that in a minute, with the others."

The living area of the house was huge. The living room was sunken with a wet bar at one end. Above the bar, another story higher, was a railing of carved wood, beyond which stretched a well-stocked library.

Joan and Benny had piled up furniture around all the windows, leaving shooting space over the top. They had secured the front door with a homemade iron brace that rested in slots hammered directly into the wall. It looked as good as he could have wanted, Meredith having done her usual thorough job.

"Listen, everybody," Bolan announced to Benny and Carver, who entered the living room just behind him and Joan. "I want to bring all of you up-to-date on the information we have so far. You, too, Ottoni. Then let's break down into specific jobs."

They all sat on a large, circular sectional couch upholstered in the ugliest shade of orange Bolan had ever seen. He looked at their somber, expectant faces, acknowledging the look and the mind-set of soldiers in combat situations.

"We've begun to put some of the pieces together." He looked at each of them in turn. "We even have some identification, thanks to Carol Niven. So far, it looks like the murders were committed by a vicious mercenary band of four men, led by a Terry Burnett. Three nights ago, Burnett was seen entering a bus station in Charlotte, North Carolina, where he retrieved a small valise from a locker. Within minutes, one of the men who was with him was found dead in a street nearby with his throat cut. Burnett is wanted by the Charlotte police for that murder. The man Carol killed in Seattle was called Cleavon Brown, a one-time Black Panther with a long police record, who seemed to thrive on petty burglaries and strong-arm assaults. He was a known associate of Burnett, as is another man we suspect of being involved—John Coolie Powell."

"I thought Villani was behind this," Ottoni said.

"We were hoping that you could help us with that one," Bolan said. "We don't know who else besides Villani would be out to get you. There is one other possibility, though. Burnett had taken out an ad in a mercenary magazine, trying to hire himself out..."

"Villani doesn't work that way." Ottoni sat up straight and shook his head. "He believes in family. He'd never go to outsiders."

"How about the leak?" Benny Young asked.

"A man named Ken Chasen is our Justice Department leak. His contact from...whoever, was a woman he called Yvette." Bolan looked at Ottoni. "Do those names mean anything to you?"

"Not a damned thing," Ottoni answered, his face showing his confusion.

Bolan sighed. "There was a fourth man with Burnett, but we don't have anything on him yet. Now, for some reason Burnett seems to have decided to leave Giancarlo for last. That means he'll hit here next. He's lost one man, which leaves three, unless they find a replacement. Each time they've hit at sundown or later with shotguns. They appear to enjoy the killing. Obviously they work for someone, but we haven't been able to trace them to Villani. When they come, I'd love to get one alive, but that's probably asking too much. The important thing here is that we stop them. Remember, after what happened in Seattle, they may be expecting us. For now I think we should leave one person on watch while the rest of us try to get some sleep, so we can be prepared to go all night tonight if we have to."

"I'll take the watch," Benny volunteered. "I couldn't sleep now anyway."

Bolan nodded. He didn't feel sleepy, either, but after being up all night he knew he needed the rest. "Okay, people," he said. "Let's get to it."

His eyes followed Ottoni, who had gone to the bar and was mixing himself an enormous drink. The man was incredibly nervous—or could it be a pretense? He was a lawyer; Bolan knew some members of the legal profession who could put on a better show in the courtroom than an actor onstage.

Bolan picked up his bag from the floor and crossed the large living room to the stairs. On the second landing Joan Meredith caught up with him.

"I'll show you where you and Roy sleep," she said, leading him down the hall to a guest room with a canopied bed and heavy oak furniture. He dropped the bag and sat heavily on the bed.

"There's still a large piece missing in this puzzle," she said, giving Bolan an inquiring look.

"You bet there is." He pulled off his shoes. "I agree with Ottoni. I don't think Villanis hired those hit men."

"Then who did?" she asked.

"The only people I can rule out are the ones already dead."

"You mean Ottoni—?"

"I don't know what I mean. Maybe Ottoni, maybe Old Sam himself... who knows? There's a game plan here that we haven't figured out yet, and that scares me."

Just then Ottoni poked his head in the door. He was carrying his drink. "Don't sleep too long," he cautioned. "Maybe they won't wait until dark this time."

He walked off, both Bolan and Meredith staring at the empty door space for a long time.

IN THE LIGHT from a sliver of moon, the Lincoln Memorial glowed like a huge light bulb against the black night sky, its white-marbled walls resembling bright sabers. Its clean healthy appearance was due in large measure to the fact that heavy industry was not allowed within the confines of Washington, D.C., so air pollution couldn't dirty this remembrance of America's possibilities and realizations.

The grounds around the memorial were left dark, unlit, so that the statue and its housing would totally rivet attention. To Ken Chasen, though, the lack of illumination was a godsend, a large area of darkness into which he could slip like a shadow, unseen. He moved through the trees of veteran's park, past the Vietnam Veterans Memorial, then down the stairs to the long, narrow reflecting pool, an adjunct to the distant Washington Monument.

He'd been on the run all day long, mingling with the tourists at all the Washington sights, seeing things he hadn't seen in ten years of working for Justice. It was so long since he'd slept he couldn't remember what it was like. His seemingly inexhaustible supply of coke was dwindling, a fact that had begun to worry him. Thank God, he'd see Yvette soon, he thought. He was living only for that moment and the salvation it would bring him.

It was cold, too cold for the T-shirt he wore. He hoped that didn't make him too conspicuous. If only he'd had enough sense to grab his wallet before he ran. At least he'd have had the money to hide himself better.

He looked at his watch, its luminous dial glowing in pulsing green. It was nearly midnight, the time he'd set with Yvette for the meet. He walked right up to the reflecting pool, kneeling to splash some of its water onto his face and hair, trying to make himself look more presentable.

He stood again, trying to ignore the few people still wandering around. He felt that all eyes were watching him, dissecting him, judging. Everyone was a stranger, all of them hostile. Earlier a man had walked up to him and asked for the time, but he was smarter than that. He had run, knowing the man was just testing him, checking to see who he was and why he was there.

A long flight of stairs led up from the pool to the memorial. He climbed the steps, crossing the asphalt drive filled with cars that was the memorial's parking section. More stairs led up to the monument itself. It was late, the regular park police who guarded the memorial by day had gone off duty, leaving only the occasional cruising patrol. Washington was a city of the people. The memorial was open twenty-four hours a day.

As he walked between the 36 Doric columns supporting the massive structure that housed the seated statue of Lincoln, he was filled with a rush of memories.

He had met Yvette at Phillips one night when he had stayed around for one more drink when the others had gone. She'd struck up a conversation with him, finally admitting that she'd only just come to town and didn't know her way around. One drink led to another, then to Chasen's gallant offer to escort the lovely lady to see the city's high points. The fact that he had been feeling less than masculine of late undoubtedly had had some influence on his intentions, but even so he had never expected what would develop. It was late, the last stop on their whirlwind tour, and the memorial was all but empty. With that wicked smile he would come to know so well, Yvette had hiked up her skirt and come on to him on the spot. Deliriously they'd made love, standing up, leaning against the statue of Lincoln.

It had been the most dizzying and exciting experience of his life. From that moment on he'd been totally devoted to her. She touched a deeply hidden, perverted chord in him that simply charged excitement back into his ordinary life. That she had asked him to meet her here tonight only reaffirmed to him the bond that held them together.

But the lights were bright in there, too bright for his dilated pupils. He wished there were some dark corner he could take shelter in. He felt so vulnerable out there in the light. He was beginning to notice the chill and needed more coke to whisk away that particular sensation.

He stood and looked up at the statue, Lincoln staring down sternly at him. He walked around to the back of the massive sculpture, to the place where their first tryst had been consummated.

Like the strength of his memory, there she stood, looking more beautiful than he'd thought possible. She was smiling, but her expression changed quickly when she saw the state he was in.

"What happened to you?" she asked, eyes narrowing.

"Oh baby." He tried to take her in his arms. "I've missed you so much."

She returned his embrace perfunctorily, then pushed him to arm's length, her face set in worry. "Tell me...what?"

He told her everything, about Marie leaving him, about the ringing phone he'd been afraid to answer, about Kaminsky and the police breaking into his house. He even told her about the doghouse. When he was finished, she stood looking at the ground, obviously deep in thought.

"You've got to help me," he begged. "I need a place to hide. I need more coke. Maybe your friends could get me out of the country."

"You're too hot," she answered coldly. "Are you sure you don't know what steps they're taking to protect the witnesses?"

"It's all fallen apart," he whined. "I've got nothing more. They know about us, Yvette. They *know*."

"But they haven't got you yet."

He wondered why her face looked so odd, so cruel. "That's why you've got to help me. You can hide me out, somehow take me—"

"They'd never allow it," she snapped. "It's all over, Ken. Once you've lost your usefulness...well, there's just nothing else to be done." She shrugged. "I guess that's how life works."

"But what about you?" he said, looking for humanity in her deep blue eyes. "What about *us*? Can't you help me? What am I supposed to do?"

Finally she smiled, reaching into her purse. "You're not supposed to do anything now, Ken...except die."

He found himself staring down the barrel of a small gun, a .32, held by a cold-looking woman he hardly recognized. "Yvette!"

He threw himself at her, the gun going off with a loud pop as he reached her. He thought he heard a scream from somewhere else in the memorial, and noticed some poor devil's blood all over the marble floor. It was only after a half minute and several abortive attempts at rising that he realized that the blood was his own.

He rolled over. The roof seemed to swirl two hundred feet above him in a mist. Then, somehow getting to his knees, he looked around for Yvette, but she was already gone. Bracing himself against the side of the statue, he staggered to his feet, leaving a streak of red on the pale white.

Blood flowed from his side, but the wound didn't seem serious, even to him. Walking was incredibly painful, though, as he tried to make his way across the floor of the monument. Several people stopped to stare in horror at him, but when a woman walked toward him, he waved her off with an angry growl.

He got outside, then tripped on the steps, rolling in a screaming ball of pain all the way to street level. He half walked, half fell across the street, his mind awash in confusion, knowing only that he needed transportation, that his weak, rubbery legs couldn't carry him very far.

As he crossed the street a Toyota Tercel with two women in the front seat pulled up and parked near him. When the driver opened her door, he threw himself on her. Screaming, she flailed at him and he responded with guttural growls and loud moans. But he managed to grab her keys away from her before letting both women run off into the night.

Cursing at his blurred vision, he fell into the front seat of the Tercel and jammed the key in the ignition, started the engine. His T-shirt was soaked in blood, but one of the women had left a heavy coat draped over the back of the seat. He ripped off his shirt and wadded it against his wound. Then he put on the too small coat and drove off.

Chasen still couldn't think. The only thing he knew was that he needed help, needed to be hidden. He remembered the addresses he had stolen from the top-secret file and had given to Yvette. One of them was in Oklahoma City. He edged the car south and gave it the gas.

BURNETT LIT A CIGARETTE and smiled at the drunken man across the table from him. They called him Big Larry. He blew a gust of stagnant breath in Burnett's face as he returned the smile through blackened and missing teeth.

"How about we kick in an extra ten bucks to make it interestin'?" Big Larry said loudly, above the pounding music, as he stuck his own cigarette in his mouth. Coolie stepped up to light it for him.

Burnett nodded and pulled another ten-dollar bill out of his pocket, slapping it down on the table, which was wet with beer. When he turned to Coolie and winked, Coolie backed away into the crowd that surrounded Burnett and Larry in the smoky, dimly lit Denver bar called the Squirrel Cage.

They had driven straight through from Seattle in the Cadillac, taking turns sleeping and driving, and had pulled in here just as soon as they saw the line of motorcycles parked in front. Nobody ever put anything over on Terry Burnett. When he went for those bastards tonight, he'd have some backup—just as soon as he finished with Big Larry.

He'd known lots of bikers and they weren't any different than soldiers. They all wore uniforms and followed orders and waged war. All you had to do was show them who was in charge.

When he looked across the table at Big Larry he knew he could take him, if for no other reason than the man was too drunk to really apply himself. Big Larry's people were called the Rogues, and they were traveling in full uniform tonight—cutoff denim jackets with their name emblazoned across the back under a pair of wings and a swastika.

"Well, I'm ready any time you are, partner," Larry said, trying to look menacing.

Burnett leaned up close, meeting the man's shifty eyes with the diamond hardness that sat in his own sockets. He puffed up his cigarette until the tip was a glowing, violent orange. "The sooner the better," he said, putting his right elbow up on the table and opening his hand.

The small crowd cheered as Big Larry brought a beefy arm up on the table and clasped Burnett's hand. One of Larry's people, a tall, thin blonde with a Vandyke and stringy hair, moved up to the table. He pulled a small length of clothesline out of his belt and tied it around the men's clasped hands.

The blond guy looked at both of them. "When I count three," he said with deadly solemnity, "get to it. The only rule is you can't use the cigarette on the face. Got it?"

"Yeah," Larry said.

"Go for it," Burnett said.

"Okay, one . . . two . . ."

Burnett puffed the cigarette hard, stoking the tip up hot.

". . . three!"

With a loud groan, the men pulled against one another, each trying to topple the other's arm. They pulled the cigarettes out of their mouths and each touched the glowing end to his adversary's arm.

The big man was stronger, levering Burnett's arm to a forty-five-degree angle almost immediately, but the moment the cigarette touched him, things changed.

Burnett had invented this variation on traditional arm wrestling while in Vietnam and hadn't been beaten at it yet. He watched Big Larry's eyes open wide in pain, some of the strength draining from his grip almost immediately.

For his part, Burnett subjugated the pain, first accepting it, then learning to live with it, then finally making love to it as the smell of roasting flesh reached his nostrils. Slashing knives of pain ran up and down his forearm even as his muscles strained against the big man, but he controlled the pain, working with it.

As the crowd yelled in approval and disbelief, Burnett played the eye game with the man, boring in, letting him know that nothing, *nothing* would make him give in.

And he pushed back, straining against a man who was giving more and more of his will over to fighting the pain.

Burnett pulled the cigarette away and puffed on it again, and his opponent regained some of his strength. But when he touched it to Larry's arm again, the fight fled from the man's eyes.

Burnett saw his opening and took it. Pressing down hard with the cigarette, he levered all his strength into his right arm, all the while maintaining the crushing eye contact. Everyone in the room knew what was going on. The two were competing in a very elemental way to see who was the better man, like rams butting heads or lions killing all the cubs of rival males in the pride.

Big Larry tried to come back, giving one last push, but Burnett could already see the retreat in his face and held firm. Larry finally gave up with a shout, his free hand coming up to rub the burns on his arms.

"You're one crazy son of a bitch, you know that?" he said as applause and cheers rang around the table.

Burnett ignored the pain in his arm, instead untying the clothesline. "Just determined," he said, picking up the wager and waving it around his head, yelling, "Beer for everybody!"

Big Larry grinned, his greasy hair hanging down in his face. He had been converted, easily sliding into the role of second best. He reached over to grab a beer right out of someone's hand, and sloshed it everywhere as he raised it in the air. "Here's to the meanest dude I ever met!"

Burnett stood, acknowledging the cheers, then pointed to Big Larry. "And here's the meanest son of a bitch *I* ever met!"

Everyone cheered wildly. Big Larry got up and took Burnett in a bear hug, both men yelling gutturally.

When the pitchers arrived they sat back down, and Coolie joined them at the table. Juke was trying to play pool nearby.

"You guys based out of Denver?" Burnett asked Big Larry as they drank.

The big man shook his head. "Colorado Springs is where the house is. We come up here a lot on weekends, though."

"You all...mind how you make your money?" Burnett asked.

Larry raised a bushy eyebrow. "What's that mean?" he asked.

Burnett sat up straight and drained his glass. "It means I got somethin' to do that I could use some help on, if you and your people don't mind how you make your money."

"How much money?" Big Larry leaned closer and lowered his voice.

"Twenty-five g's," Burnett replied casually.

"That's thousand? Twenty-five thousand?" The man gestured theatrically. "Who do I have to kill?"

"His name isn't important," Burnett answered, giving the biker a hard stare.

"You're serious?"

Burnett nodded. "About the bread *and* about the dude."

The man sat quietly for a minute, then took another sip of beer. "Where's the money?"

Burnett unbuttoned his fatigue shirt pocket and pulled out the wad of hundred-dollar bills, dropping it on the table in front of Larry. "Put it in your pocket," he invited. "See how it feels."

Larry looked around quickly, then scooped up the wad and stuffed it in his pocket. "What's the gig?"

"There's a man, a lawyer, who lives out at Big Bear Lake," Coolie explained. "He needs to die, and we need some help killing him."

"If you and your people are man enough," Burnett added, "the money's yours."

Big Larry sucked air through his teeth. "You know, a big shipment of coke just showed up in town. With twenty-five grand, I could buy and turn twice that."

"A good couple hours' work," Coolie replied.

"What the hell." Larry got to his feet. "C'mon outside. Got somethin' I want to show you."

Burnett stood, laying a hand on Coolie's shoulder. "Stay put," he said, then leaned down to whisper in his ear. "If I ain't back in five minutes come out and look for me."

Coolie nodded and poured himself another beer, while Burnett walked through the crowded bar and out into the cold Denver night with Big Larry.

"Quite a deal running into you tonight," Larry remarked as he led Burnett down the long line of chopped Harleys. "We made a big score on smokin' dope a few days ago and just spent it all." He came to a stop at the back of a nondescript van painted primer gray.

"What'd you spend it all on?" Burnett asked.

"This," the biker answered, unlocking the van and pulling open the back door.

The floor of the van was filled with hardware—submachine guns and cases of ammo, high-powered rifles, handguns and a crate full of grenades, including a launcher.

The two men looked at each other in understanding. "Let's party," Big Larry said.

10

Ottoni couldn't stop pacing. He walked continuously, peering nervously out one window, then moving on to the next. The only time he stopped his perpetual rounds was when he went to the bar to mix himself another drink, which happened with regularity every fifteen minutes.

"Ottoni's tearing himself up," Joan Meredith said as she and Bolan watched him pass the couch where they were sitting to go to the bar again. "He's going to go to pieces if something doesn't happen soon."

"I should have got the booze out of here," Bolan replied. "The way he's soaking it up, he couldn't help us out if his life depended upon it."

"And it probably does," Meredith added.

Ottoni finished mixing a tall drink at the bar and walked back to sit opposite them on the circular couch. "I can't stand this waiting," he complained. "We've got to do something. Isn't there some way to find out..."

"We are doing something," Bolan said. "We're waiting."

"Maybe I was wrong to insist on staying put," Ottoni said. "Maybe moving out is the best course. Maybe you should drive me somewhere else."

"It's too late for that now," Bolan told him. "We're committed. Just relax . . . trust my judgment."

"I don't even know who the hell you are." The steady intake of alcohol made Ottoni slur his words slightly. "Why should I trust you?"

Bolan just stared at him and changed the subject. "The guards at the main gate, what do they know about all this? Are they expecting trouble?"

"They know everything," Ottoni replied swiftly. "It's taken care of."

Bolan eyed him suspiciously. The way Ottoni had answered him so quickly, his defensiveness, made the Executioner wonder if the man was telling the truth or not. He was about to follow his suspicion when the walkie-talkie on the sofa beside him squawked loudly. Then Roy Carver's voice came booming through the static. "Belasko. Come in. Over."

Bolan picked up the receiver, and spoke into it. "This is Belasko. What's wrong? Over."

"Maybe nothing," Carver returned. "I'm not sure. I want you to come up here and check if you could."

"I'll be right there." Bolan shut down the instrument without even signing off. Turning to Meredith, he stood and said, "Everybody on alert. Get to your places just in case. Ottoni, hide somewhere."

He left the house through the door to the patio. The ladder leading up to the first level of roof was set firmly on the concrete of the patio. He hurried up it, the chill of the night slicing right into him.

He reached the first roof level. The house was tiered up this high, with five or six different flat roofs butting up against one another. He climbed from roof to roof, meeting Roy Carver atop the highest. The sky was magnificent all around them, with no bright city lights to cover up the multitude of stars poking through the curtain of black that stretched to infinity. From up here they had an unhampered view not only of Ottoni's neighborhood, but of the entire lake and the surrounding countryside for miles.

"What have you got?" he asked Carver.

"Shapes," Carver replied, taking off his binoculars and pointing with them in the direction of the roadway. "I think something's moving. After a while your eyes start playing tricks on you and *everything* looks like it's moving."

Bolan took the field glasses from him, and stared through them in the direction that Carver had pointed. He saw nothing but darkness at ground level. Without city lights, the vista that was so magnificent during the day created nothing but problems for one trying to stand watch.

Then he saw movement, just a glimpse of movement, like the shadow of an airplane flitting quickly across the ground a couple miles distant. It almost seemed as if there were dark forms moving at street level—a lot of dark forms. More than seemed reasonable. If only he could get some definition. He pulled the glasses down, straining his eyes and his ears in that direction, wishing for an infrared scope.

"What do you—"

"Shh. Listen."

He could see nothing, but a sound was reaching him just on the edge of his range of hearing, a small sound, like a fly buzzing. No—more than one fly, a swarm.

"Get down and get into position," Bolan said, handing him back the glasses. "Something's up. I think they're coming in without headlights."

"This is it?" Carver said.

Bolan looked hard at him. "Shoot to kill," he said.

The Executioner ran the length of the roof, jumping from level to level, then climbing down the ladder. Once again, the method of attack had changed. Unless he missed his guess, they were coming in on motorcycles—and there were a lot more than three of them.

He hurried into the house. Running into the living room he saw Joan armed with a MAC-10 SMG, a bandolier of extra clips wrapped around her shoulder, hair tied back out of the way.

"This is it," Bolan announced. "Is Benny on alert?"

"He's in position," Meredith answered, pulling out her clip to check the load, then snapping it back into place. "How many?"

"Might be a bunch, coming in without lights."

Ottoni stood by the bar, frozen, staring, mouth open. "Th-they're...really coming?" he whispered, his face drained of color.

Bolan nodded. "Are the guys at the gate supposed to notify us if they spot trouble?"

The man looked confused. "Yeah...no...hell, I don't know what..."

"Did you warn them what was happening?" Bolan demanded, striding across the room to face the man.

Ottoni's eyes shifted. As he raised his glass to his lips, Bolan slapped it out of his hand and it shattered against the bar.

"Did you warn them?" he repeated loudly.

The man just stared at him.

"You set those people up to die," Bolan yelled, "just to keep your name a secret."

"So what?" Ottoni finally said, leaning against the bar for support. "Who gives a damn about them?"

Bolan grabbed the guy's shirtfront, slamming him against the bar. "Where's the phone number for the gate?" he demanded.

"On the p-pad next to the phone." Ottoni pointed to the kitchen. Then he slipped to the floor and rolled over on his hands and knees, throwing up on the carpet.

Bolan ran to the kitchen, passing Carver on the way in. The man was carrying the ladder he'd used to get on the roof. "Secure the patio door!" Bolan yelled.

He ran to the ktichen phone. The pad was filled with emergency phone numbers. Running his finger down the list he at last found the number for the front gate. As he ripped the receiver off the hook, he hoped he wasn't too late.

BURNETT LED THE PROCESSION in his white Cadillac. Big Larry's van was close behind, followed by twelve motorcycles riding two abreast. About a block from the fancy neighborhood Burnett stopped to look over the layout.

"Quite the place," Coolie commented from the passenger seat.

"Yeah," Burnett replied, excited at the prospect of screwing up some rich bastard. "And it looks like the front door's the only way in. Sit tight for a minute."

He climbed out of the car and walked back to Big Larry's van.

Larry rolled down his window and poked his head out. He had a beer can in his hand. "What's up, brother?" he asked.

"Wait here while I take out the security guard," Burnett told him. "When we go in, let's kill the bike motors until we're almost there. No point in giving them early warning."

Larry smiled. "You're the man." He climbed out of the van to go back to talk to his people. The bikers carried twenty-five thousand dollars in half bills, the other half in Burnett's pocket for safekeeping until the job was finished.

Burnett got back in the Cadillac and turned to the back seat to face Juke. "I want you to do me a favor."

The man brightened. "Sure, Burnett."

"I'm going to drive up and talk to the man in the guardhouse. I want you to help me shut him up...quietly."

Juke smiled, nodding his head with enthusiasm. "I can do that. Sure I can do that."

Burnett turned and started the car, knowing that the Cadillac would get him right up to the gate of a place like this, no sweat.

Slowly he drove up to the gate, where a man barely out of his teens put down a book and opened the sliding window to poke his head out. "Can I help you?" he asked.

"Yeah," Burnett replied as Juke opened the back door on the side farthest from the security man and slipped out quietly. The guard didn't even notice the simpleminded mercenary as he crept around the back of the vehicle. "I'm trying to get to Red Rock Park," Burnett continued, "and I think I've gone too far."

"You came down the canyon road?"

"Sure."

Juke crouched by the rear bumper, waiting for the man to look away.

"Well, I don't know how you could have missed the cutoff," the guard said. "It's right after you pass Morrison—" A phone in the guardhouse rang. He broke off at the sound, saying, "Just a minute..."

As he turned to answer the phone, Juke sprang up, grabbing him by the arm resting on the windowsill and pulling. Yelping in surprise, the guard was yanked right through the window into Burnett's lap. His shoulder hit the horn, which blared loudly. Burnett swore, pushing at the struggling man to get him off the horn. "The Ka-bar!" he yelled to Coolie. Coolie reached to the floor and ripped the knife out of Burnett's boot.

The phone continued ringing while the man flopped like a grounded fish. He managed to get in a weak punch to Burnett's stomach. The mercenary boss bashed him on the side of the head with his free hand.

"Knife!" Coolie yelled. Burnett snatched the weapon, and immediately plunged the point in the guard's ear and pushed down hard.

The guard jerked spasmodically, blood gushing up out of the ear like a fountain. In seconds it was all over. The guard jerked several times, then lay still.

"God, what a friggin' mess." Burnett looked at the blood all over his hands, arms and clothes. Juke pulled the body out of the car and slid it back into the guardhouse.

The phone finally stopped ringing.

Burnett climbed out of the car to operate the controls for the gate through the guardhouse window. The gate opened smoothly and he drove in, followed by Big Larry and his people.

The procession moved quietly down the street, then stopped in front of the gate leading into the pigeon's house. Like most of the houses in the neighborhood, the place was dark.

"Looks like they don't want no company." Juke laughed. Burnett turned to look at Coolie. "Go back and unload the grenades. We'll blast through that gate."

ALL OVER THE HOUSE lights were being turned off as Bolan listened to the phone ringing unanswered in the guardhouse. At last he hung up and took a deep breath. They were in the neighborhood.

He turned off the light by the phone, then walked through the spacious kitchen. Carver had turned a table on its side and shoved it up against the patio door, then piled chairs against the table. He was squatted behind the breakfast bar armed with an Uzi SMG and a stack of extra clips. "They're through the gates," Bolan told him. "Keep low."

In the living room, Benny Young crouched behind a small bookcase that had been pushed up against the window. He held a shotgun, and a .38 lay beside him on the carpet. "Make it count, Benny." Bolan put a hand on the man's shoulder. "They'll be easy targets if you take your time."

Joan Meredith stood in the blackness of the formal dining room just off the living room. A breakfront had been pushed against the window, blocking it except for a space at one side, no wider than a foot, for her to shoot through.

"They're out there," she told Bolan when he walked up. "I thought I saw one of them messing around the gate."

"I don't know how many there are, but it's more than three. Where's Ottoni?"

She shook her head, looking around. "I don't know. Hope he hasn't gone for a walk."

Bolan eased his Beretta out of its harness and released the safety. He looked through the window across fifteen feet of artificial turf to the front gate.

The darkness in the house was all-pervading, mood-altering, as shadows took on substance and the atmosphere of fear grew stronger. He hated the waiting. If they were coming, let them come on. They just needed to—

An explosion rocked the front gate, orange light flared and a rush of white smoke blew across the lawn like dirty fog.

"This is it!" Bolan yelled as engines roared to life outside and headlights glared. Motorcycles screamed through the gate, emerging like one-eyed monsters from the smoke haze.

"Fire!" the Executioner shouted as he took out the first man through the vapor with a clean shot from the Beretta. Immediately automatic fire raked the front of the house, driving him and Meredith back, the curtains dancing as 9 mm slugs tore up the breakfront, smashing dishes and splintering the walls all around.

The volley died. Bolan and Meredith were up again, firing. The yard was filled with screaming bikes and screaming men. Benny began shooting from the living room, cursing loudly as he fired. A bike buzzed the house. Meredith unseated the rider with a burst from the Ingram. The cycle ran up on the porch and smashed into the front door, shattering it except for the massive iron bar.

Return fire was minimal, and Bolan wondered why as he picked another target in the buzzing confusion.

He took the rider at head level, blasting through helmet and bone to scatter brains all over the yard. Then he saw the reason for the quiet guns.

"Grenades!" he yelled. "Get down!"

He hit the floor, pulling Joan with him as objects began bouncing off the walls and porch like hailstones.

There was a second of dead silence, then the whole world came apart in blinding flashes, falling objects and earsplitting rumbles. Large sections of the front of the house blew inward, debris and plaster dust choking up all visibility. The chandelier fell from the dining room ceiling on top of Bolan and Meredith. The breakfront disintegrated in pieces all around them.

Bolan pushed the chandelier off them and rolled to his feet. The house was unrecognizable, a jumble of destruction and floating plaster dust. Small fires blazed here and there in the haze, contributing to the choking atmosphere.

Again the cycles roared outside. They rode directly at the house, bouncing up the porch and entering through the holes in the wall. The bikers fired wildly from the hip as they drove in.

Benny was up, returning fire. Bolan and Meredith joined him. One . . . two men fell from their bikes, the big machines skidding crazily across the floor to smash into the wall.

Bolan charged through the alien landscape, firing at shadows in the dust- and smoke-filled house. In the sunken living room he leveled a shot at a denim-clad back. The rider jerked in his seat and his bike ran full speed into the wet bar, smashing in two. A ruptured water pipe spouted a fountain into the air.

"In here!" Roy Carver called from the kitchen as Bolan fired up at the open library above. One of the punks took 9 mm death at chest level and fell forward over the railing with a scream, landing crumpled atop the corpse and motorcycle already tangled up in the remnants of the bar.

Bolan fought his way to the kitchen. Roy Carver, bleeding from several wounds, was busy reloading his Uzi as a huge man burst through the glass of the patio door, shoving the table and chairs out of his way as he went.

Carver snapped the clip and fired at the man, whose torso exploded in bloody froth. But the oxlike punk continued lumbering forward, grabbing the cursing Carver and lifting him over his head, all the while screaming without words.

Bolan launched himself like a missile, hitting the big man at knee level. Knocked off balance, the giant buckled beneath Carver's weight, and crashed to the floor. But he had breached the defenses, and motorcycles now charged through the opening created by the huge mercenary.

Carver was up on his knees, pounding the big ox's face with his gun butt. Bolan rolled away, firing at the men coming in. He took out the first with a head shot from the Beretta. The man's face exploded. He fell beneath the wheels of his bike as it bounced over him, continuing riderless into the living room.

The next bike came right at Bolan, the rider going up on one wheel as Bolan tried to aim.

"Watch out!" Bolan called to Carver as the bike roared toward them. The driver jumped at Bolan. Carver rolled to the side just in time, as the bike fell atop the giant. The hot pipes crashed into the bruiser's face, and his life drained away in gurgling screams as Bolan caught the rider in mid-jump. The two of them slammed into the linoleum floor, with the Executioner on top.

The biker cocked a beefy fist, but before he could connect, Bolan lashed out with a stiff arm and open palm to the base of the punk's nose, driving the cartilage straight back into his brain. His mouth and eyes rolled back crazily, and his mouth gaped wide. Blood bubbled out of his ears, nose and mouth. In seconds, he was gone.

"Roy!" Bolan called.

Carver waved weakly to him from the kitchen. "I'm okay!"

Bolan jumped up as another bike shot through the wrecked door, and ripped Big Thunder out of his webbing.

In the dining room Meredith and Benny Young worked the cross fire, blasting dark forms moving through the smoke, laying out a stack of bodies. Then Benny yelled as a biker jumped him and they grappled in a hand-to-hand fight.

His cry distracted Meredith's attention for only a second. She had taken one step in his direction, when an arm flashed out from behind the wreck of the breakfront, slamming her viciously across the face. She blacked out for a second, then felt herself falling. Excruciating pain shot through her whole body as she hit the wall and went down in a heap on the floor. Stunned, confused, she looked up to see the ghoulish form of a skinhead, picking his way toward her through the smoking debris. He wore old army fatigues and half gloves, and he held a knife with a bloody blade in his hands.

"Oh...you're mine, bitch," he cooed, and his tone, almost sexual, made Meredith shudder. His eyes were glazed, and his tongue kept licking dry lips. A thin layer of plaster dust had settled on him, giving him a ghastly, spectral appearance. In her confusion, with the fires and the smoke and devastation all around, she felt that she could have been in hell.

Shakily she got to her feet, her weapons lost somewhere in the madness. The man stalked her slowly, delighting in her fear the way a cat savors its kill beforehand. He was barely four feet from her now. He changed the blade from hand to hand as he smiled wickedly.

"I'm gonna do you, lady," he rasped. "I'm gonna do you real slow."

She caught his eyes, saw the madness there. Her mind hardened, falling back on her years of training and her instinct. If she went down, it would be after giving this son of a bitch the fight of his life.

She continued to watch his eyes and when they flashed again, she threw herself at him just as he lunged for her. She hit him in the chest, pushing him back into the breakfront. The punk groaned in surprise as he fell among the shelves full of shattered dishes and glasses.

He went half to his knees before recovering and straightening. All over his face and arms were cuts from broken glass. He put a hand to his cheek, bringing the fingers to his eyes to stare in fascination at his own blood. Then, without warning, he charged, screaming like a banshee.

Meredith turned away, meeting his force with a braced elbow, then twirled around and followed through with a left to the nose. He grunted, then slammed her with a hard right hand to the chin, knocking her backward to trip over a broken chair and fall to the floor.

Blood flowed freely from the biker's nose, running all over his face and chest as he threw himself at her. Meredith twisted away. He landed hard beside her. She cracked the side of his head with her other elbow, scrambled to her feet and grabbed the chair she had fallen over.

She raised the chair, bringing it down with all her strength over his back as he tried to rise. He was driven to one knee, but the chair had not been heavy enough to do serious damage.

He came up making animal sounds, his face twisted in a maniacal leer. His hand lashed out, grabbing her arm and slinging her against the wall.

"Aaahh!" She hit hard. Strength drained from her.

He hobbled forward. "Now, bitch," he murmured in triumph. "Now!" He threw himself at her. Meredith responded with a last desperate kick to the groin.

She hit him just right. He doubled over and gagged. She grabbed him by the hair and raised her knee, brought his face down hard onto the knee. She could hear his teeth and nose breaking as the skinhead sank to the floor.

She fell on top of him, breathing hard. Instinctively she reached for a large shard of glass amid the rubble.

"Bitch!" he groaned. "Goddamn whore!"

She didn't know how many women this man had caused pain to in his life, but she knew there had been plenty and that he'd never do it again. She raised the glass, even as the punk began struggling against her again, and plunged it into his throat, tearing.

With his remaining strength, the man bucked her off and tried to stand. Instead he lurched sideways and collapsed to finally bleed to death in the plaster dust that covered the floor.

She looked up. Benny Young was standing at the edge of the dining room, his face scratched and bleeding, his shirt ripped from his body. His .38 was clutched in his hand, its butt dripping thick globs of blood. The hoodlum he'd been struggling with had just lost his last battle.

He nodded to Joan and, reassured she was okay, moved into the next room.

In the kitchen, meanwhile, three more members of Larry's motorcycle gang ran in from the patio, firing as they came. They drove Bolan back through the archway to the living room. The Sheetrock walls collapsed under the withering machine gun fire.

After the first volley, the Executioner spun around with Big Thunder on automatic, just as Carver aimed the .45 over the breakfast bar. They pounded away unmercifully, tearing up the first two men, who danced a jerky mazurka as they fell, the flesh ripped from their bodies.

The third man turned and ran, jumping back through the patio door. Bolan gave chase. He arrived outside as the punk was firing a motorcycle.

Bolan raised Big Thunder and fired, the hammer falling on an empty chamber as the cycle started to roared away. Looking down, Bolan spied Roy's ladder half in, half out of the patio door. He picked it up and threw it. The ladder hit the front wheel of the bike and knocked it sideways, throwing the rider off.

He picked himself up and ran across the back lawn toward the pier, with Bolan close behind.

The man charged the length of the small dock, jumping into the boat and untying it. As Bolan reached the dock, the punk shoved hard and the boat floated gently out into the lake.

Bolan, still carrying Big Thunder, ran to the end of the pier. The enemy was already ten feet out, too far for Bolan to make a jump for it.

The punk pulled the starter rope, the outboard motor kicking over on the second try.

Bolan popped the clip out of the AutoMag and dug down in his webbing for another as the mercenary laughed loudly and sped off in a wild cascade of water.

Bolan shoved the new clip into the automatic and advanced a round into the chamber.

The punk was fifty feet away now, his shrill laughter echoing across the water.

With stiff arms Bolan extended Big Thunder, sighting along the high, arcing wake created by the powerful engine as the boat moved quickly into the darkness. The Executioner fired on single shot, one after another, recalculating speed and position with every squeeze of the trigger. Slowly and methodically he emptied the entire clip.

The sound of the engine changed slightly then, revved higher. Bolan dropped the clip from the AutoMag and reached for another, while his eyes searched the blackness of the lake for any sight of the boat.

Then he heard it coming back, its whine louder, closer. He shoved in the new clip and raised the gun again. The boat was making a large circle, dipping in about thirty feet from the pier. It looped once, twice, then suddenly straightened course and came right at Bolan.

The Executioner aimed Big Thunder again, watching in fascination as the boat bore down on him at high speed. Then he realized that the boat wasn't coming toward him at all, that it was going to miss the pier completely.

At last he understood. He lowered his gun. The speedboat screamed in, a dead man at the wheel. It rushed past the pier, spraying water that soaked Bolan where he stood.

Then it hit the seawall at the end of the lawn, and disintegrated on impact. The body of Coolie Powell was thrown out of the boat, flew gracefully across the lawn and finally landed with a loud plop on the flat roof of the house.

Bolan turned and looked at the house. Smoke poured through the windows, and the flames of small fires flickered. But there were no more gunshots, no explosions. He heard sirens in the background, neighbors apparently having called in the police.

He moved back across the lawn, surprised to feel a soreness in his right leg that he hadn't noticed before. He stopped by the door from the patio to the kitchen, where the dead man sprawled half off the roof. Bolan reached up and pulled his queue, and the body toppled off the roof, to land like a sack of garbage on the patio.

Roy Carver was walking around in the smoky kitchen, checking bodies, his left arm hanging limp at his side, his clothes soaked in blood.

"You okay?" Bolan asked.

He nodded grimly. "Nothing a few stitches won't fix up." He pointed to the tough ox who lay dead under the motorcycle. "I think this is one of the ones who killed Neal and Carol."

Bolan pulled some wood debris off the body and looked at it, nodding. "We've got another one out on the patio," he said. "You sit down and take it easy. We'll get you to a hospital."

"Hey, listen. I'm fine, I . . ."

"Just do what I tell you," Bolan said, moving out of the kitchen and into the living room.

The place was a shambles, sofas overturned, their stuffing floating in the air like snow. A small fire was burning in the wreckage of the Harley that had crashed onto the bar, most of it contained thanks to the broken water pipe. A blue-suited policeman ran into the room with a fire extinguisher, ignoring Bolan to hurry to the bar.

Benny Young stood talking to several policemen, showing identification all around, a job that Bolan was more than happy to let him handle himself. The way bodies were piled up around the front door area, Benny and Joan had done a hell of a job.

Joan Meredith sat on a three-legged stool near the entrance to the dining room as a white-jacketed ambulance attendant applied antiseptic to a small gash on her face. Several other attendants in white coats moved among the bodies, checking for any signs of life.

Bolan walked up to Joan. She reached up to take his hand. "We've got a man down in the kitchen," he told the attendant just as he was about to apply a bandage to Joan's cheek. "Get someone to take care of him."

The man nodded, accepting Bolan's tone of authority. He put down sterile gauze and tape and turned away to give orders to the stretcher bearers. Joan got up from the stool.

"You okay?" he asked.

She nodded. Her face was streaked with plaster, soot and blood. Bolan figured he probably looked the same. "I think I got Burnett in there," she said, inclining her head toward the dining room.

Bolan walked in there, grunting when he saw from all the wreckage how fierce the fighting in the dining room had been. He knelt beside the body with the slashed throat, knowing right away it was Burnett. After rolling the body over he fished through the pockets, coming out with a wad of bills torn in half and a key ring. He tossed the money down and took the keys.

He went back to Meredith, who was sitting down again and wearing a large bandage on her cheek. Though her face was still pale, she seemed to be in pretty good shape. "Find an open phone," he told her. "Get Hal on the line...now."

Without a question, she walked off, obviously pleased to have been given a job to do. Bolan passed a couple more policemen going in the house as he came out.

There were several more fires on the lawn, caused by motorcycle crashes and pieces from the outside of the house. Several more bodies lay strewed around the scene of destruction. The arrival of the police had drawn a group of neighbors, who gathered outside the gate to gawk and offer theories.

Bolan picked his way through the twisted wreckage of the gate, glaring at any neighbors who were bold enough to approach him. He approached the white Cadillac parked on the street, heading straight for the trunk, which he opened with a key from Burnett's ring.

A Colorado highway patrolman walked up as he rooted through the duffel bag containing shotgun and ammo.

"I don't know who the hell you are," he said as Bolan dropped the duffel bag and reached for the valise jammed far in the back, "but you've done us quite a favor. The damned Rogues have been a thorn in our sides for years."

Bolan looked up, met the man's eyes, nodded once and resumed his search. He unzipped the valise, dumping the contents into the trunk.

Banded stacks of money fell from the suitcase, a lot of money. Ignoring it, he picked up the manila envelope in the middle of the pile. It contained a list of addresses for Vito Perezzi, Stinky Barberi and Mario Ottoni, and photos of all three. That was it. Old Sam wasn't even on this dude's list.

Puzzled by this turn of events, he tossed the envelope back into the trunk and closed it. As he walked slowly back to the house, he met ambulance attendants carrying Roy Carver across the front lawn on a stretcher.

"Good work, Roy," he said, stopping the attendants for a moment. "You'll make a great agent."

The man smiled weakly, the morphine they'd given him for the pain already working. "Had a good teacher," he whispered, taking Bolan's hand. "Thanks."

Bolan smiled. "Get better," he said.

Joan Meredith was waiting for him in the house when he walked in. "I've got Hal on the kitchen phone," she said. "He's anxious to talk with you."

"Good." He made his way through the ever-growing crowds of police and medics. As he picked up the phone in the kitchen, he wondered idly if Meredith had charged the call to Ottoni or put it on the government number. It seemed to him that Ottoni should pay for something. And where the hell *was* Ottoni?

"Yeah, Hal," he said.

"I hear it got rough," Brognola said. "Is everybody on the team okay?"

"Just minor injuries," Bolan replied, "cuts and bruises. No harm done."

"How about Ottoni?"

"He went off to hide somewhere," Bolan answered. "I was just wondering about him."

"Did any of them get away?" the Fed asked.

"I don't think so. We got the three who killed Lomax and Niven. I found out from a cop outside that they recruited a local biker gang to help them on this one."

"Then you got all of them?" Brognola asked.

"All that we know about," Bolan qualified. "That doesn't mean—"

"Then let's shut the door on this son of a bitch and call it a day. You did a great job, Mack."

Bolan ran a hand across his forehead, his fingers coming away streaked with black. "It's not that simple, Hal," he said. "There's something more going on. Who hired these punks? Why haven't they hit Old Sam yet?''

"Don't worry about it," Brognola replied. "I don't get you. From minute one you haven't wanted anything to do with this project. Now that I'm giving you an out, a free pass away, you don't want to take it."

"I just can't leave the job unfinished after all that's happened," Bolan explained. "There's more to this than meets the eye and we need to figure out why."

"What are you telling me?"

"I'm going back to Oklahoma to get to the bottom of this."

"Leave it alone, Mack." There was more than a little exasperation in Brognola's voice. "They're not that happy with you at Old Sam's house—you *did* punch out his kid—and as far as I can see up here, the thing's a wrap. Why not just forget it?"

"You know what I think, Hal? I think you're afraid Old Sam is somehow mixed up in this himself and you don't want me screwing up your grand jury indictments over it."

"That's not true," Brognola said quietly.

"All right then," Bolan countered. "If Old Sam isn't tied up in it, then his life is still in danger. I found a suitcase full of money in Burnett's trunk, and whoever had that kind of money to pay off a punk like that will have a lot more to hire other punks."

The line was quiet a minute. Bolan watched three cops pull the motorcycle off the big guy on the floor so the attendants could get a stretcher under him. Finally Brognola spoke. "You win," he said. "Take a couple of more days down there...take Joanie with you if she wants to go. But if nothing is happening, don't make a career out of it."

"Don't worry. I won't spend any more time with the Giancarlo family than I absolutely have to. Talk to you later."

Bolan hung up the phone and walked back toward the living room where Benny was still busy with the police, making statements and showing credentials. He met Joan as she came downstairs, a puzzled expression on her face.

"Is something wrong up there?" he asked.

"I'm not sure," she replied. "It's Ottoni. I can't find him anywhere. The bathroom door is locked, but nobody answers when I knock."

"Let's take a look." Bolan followed the woman up the stairs, noticing that this part of the house was relatively untouched.

"It's off the master bedroom," she said over her shoulder as she led the way down the narrow, carpeted hall.

They turned into a large bedroom, furnished with light-colored woods and decorated in earth tones. Joan knocked loudly on the bathroom door. "Mr. Ottoni?" she called. "Are you in there?"

No answer.

She tried again. Still no answer. The niceties out of the way, Bolan stepped up, lifted his foot and kicked at the door, then again, until it shattered at the frame and came open.

They entered the bathroom and looked down. Ottoni lay on the floor, eyes open wide, arms outstretched in the martyr's pose. Great gashes in his wrists gaped open, blood all over the white tile floor. A razor blade lay at the edge of the pool of blood.

Suicide.

11

Ken Chasen sat in the car for several minutes at the Nashville gas station before getting out. He just didn't know what to do. There was no time now—no time to think, to plan. Everything, including his head, was moving at double time. He was weak, he knew that, and would have to eat sometime. People were after him, he knew that, too. But his most immediate concern was he was out of gas again and had to figure out some way of getting some without any money.

He opened the tight-fitting women's coat and looked at himself in the harsh yellow light of the combination self-service gas bar and convenience store. The T-shirt tied around his gut was no more than a dark, soaked rag, though he thought the bleeding had stopped, leaving behind a throbbing pain that just got worse and worse. Why had Yvette shot him? If only she had listened, he could have explained to her the situation he was in. He'd been wrestling with this question all night, over and over, to the exclusion of everything else, as he continued his headlong flight across a country that had turned dark and sinister to him.

Maybe she hadn't really shot him. Maybe the gun had gone off accidentally when he grabbed for her. Maybe she had been scared herself and hadn't known what to do. If only she had stayed around, he could have explained to her that together they could accomplish anything. He could still reach her. It wasn't too late. All he had to do was find her friends and explain it to them. They were professionals; they'd understand and be able to deal with this sort of thing. He could go to work for them. Surely a sharp legal mind like his with an understanding of the Justice Department would come in handy. Sure. That was it. What was he worrying about?

Gas. Gas was what he was worried about. He needed gas and he needed food. At the last gas stop he had ferreted around in the car and found enough in a toll booth can in the glove compartment to fill the tank. But now that was gone. He *had* to fill the tank again. It was a matter of life-and-death. Surely anyone working at a place like this would understand. But if they didn't understand, where would he be? He'd just have to take what he needed and hope they'd understand later. That was it. It was the right thing, the only thing, to do. None of this was his fault. None of it.

He climbed out of the car, wrapped the coat around himself and managed to button it, though the sleeves came up nearly to his elbows. He moved around to the pump, setting the handle in the automatic notch after sticking the nozzle in the tank.

The entrance to the convenience store was about twenty feet from the pumps. He walked casually toward it, making sure no one else was lurking around watching.

"Howdy," the man behind the counter said. He was a man in his late fifties wearing bib overalls and a checked flannel shirt, and reading the morning paper while puffing on a big briar pipe.

"Morning," Chasen mumbled, sizing the man up. He was small and old and the only person around. This would work out just fine.

Chasen moved into the guts of the place. A Moe Bandy song was playing on the radio at the counter. He turned down the junk food aisle, immediately filling his pockets with cupcakes, chips and cookies. He wasn't hungry, hadn't been for days, but he knew he had to eat. A deep pain was gnawing away at his gut and food would relieve it. For Ken Chasen life had become an elemental game of survival.

He slid open the door of a glass-fronted refrigerator case and grabbed a sandwich encased in plastic wrap and as many cans of Coke as he could carry. Then he walked past the counter and headed for the door.

"Hey, young fella..." the old storekeeper called to him.

"Back in a minute," he said as he hurried through the door, letting it close behind him.

Then he picked up the pace, noticing how the glow of the slowly rising sun lent the landscape a stark beauty. He opened the passenger door and dropped his handfuls of food into the seat, then went around to the gas pump.

"Hold on there," came the old man's voice.

Damn. The son of a bitch had followed him outside. Chasen hastily pulled the nozzle from the tank as the old man rushed up and pointed his pipe at him.

"You haven't paid for any of that stuff you took," he accused.

Chasen turned to him. "I told you I'd be right back."

"Look," the storekeeper said, angry now. "It's laying in your car. You'd better pay me right now, or I'm calling the cops."

Chasen jerked toward him. His hands tightened involuntarily on the nozzle control, and gasoline shot out of the nozzle to drench the old man.

"Hey!" the man yelled and jumped back, his pipe falling to the ground.

It all happened in an instant. The pipe bounced off the old man's shoe, embers spilling, immediately igniting the gas dripping from his body.

The old man went up like a match, blazing brightly, nearly blinding Chasen, who stood watching in rapt fascination as the man spun away from the pumps, his hands covering his face, his screams shrill and loud, so incredibly loud.

Dropping the nozzle, Chasen jumped into the car, gas still running out across the concrete drive. As he turned on the ignition, he watched the old fellow in the rearview mirror still moving in circles, screaming, his body already a blackened twig.

Chasen pulled out quickly. The incinerated man finally fell to the ground, the stream of gas from the nozzle inching ever nearer to him. While the fugitive accelerated away down the service road, the line of fire ran from the dying man back to the nozzle, then to the tanks, setting off a monstrous explosion. The gas pumps shot into the morning sky like Saturn rockets, the entire station a huge orange ball of fire. Chasen steered the stolen Toyota up the ramp to the interstate.

He looked at his watch. He still had a long way to go, a lot of driving to do. Why couldn't the old guy have left him alone, instead of making all that trouble over a few bucks worth of gas and groceries. It wasn't Chasen's fault. The old man had brought an accident upon himself because of his greed. His damned filthy greed.

Chasen picked up the sandwich, bringing it to his mouth and ripping at the plastic with his teeth until it opened. He stuffed an entire half sandwich into his mouth, slowly chewing on the big wad. Food, that was what he had needed. He'd be fine after he ate. If only the lines dividing the highway lanes would stop wriggling like snakes.

"I DON'T LIKE THIS whole deal," Tony Ferrari said as he drove north on Lincoln Boulevard. The Oklahoma state capitol building stood right in the middle of the street several blocks distant, with a large oil derrick pumping away right on its front lawn. "I mean, why do we have to keep putting Rocco off about how this is goin' down?"

Vic D'matto sat beside Tony, watching the mixed bag of whores who were plying their trade up and down the streets, all of them dressed to the teeth in the middle of a dull afternoon. "We're saying nothing because that's the way the old man wants it," he returned. He could tell from the number of girls on the street that they were all free-lancers. Somebody needed to get in here and organize them.

"I heard that," Ferrari said. "I been hearin' that since we left Joliet, but that don't mean nothin' to me, you know?"

"You may be my brother-in-law, Tony," D'matto said with a sigh, "but you're just a punk. You need to develop a little respect. The old man's been good to us, you know? What the shit does it matter—if he asks us to keep our mouths shut, we keep our fucking mouths shut, that's all."

"But don't you wonder..."

"No, I don't wonder." Angry now, Vic turned to face the younger man. "In our business it doesn't pay to wonder. You do your job, you look straight ahead, and you don't wonder about anything. You just do what you're told. Period."

"Okay, okay! Don't get all hot and bothered." Ferrari flicked a fingernail across the bottom of his front teeth. "I just don't know what the hell we tell Rocco when he keeps askin'."

"We tell him to ask his old man, that's what," Vic said. His eyes dropped to the small suitcase at his feet. He wouldn't admit it to Ferrari, but he wondered, too. There was something about the whole setup that had smelled from minute one. The old man was a thinker, a planner, and this deal had to be part of some big plan that Vic hadn't been able to figure out yet. He just hoped that he wasn't an expendable part of that plan.

"Well, I'll just be happy to get this deal out of the way so we can get back to the south side." Ferrari turned the rented car into the parking lot of the Best Western motel just a block from the capitol. "Being out here in the sticks ain't exactly my idea of a good time."

"Mine, either, pal." Vic picked up the suitcase and set it in his lap. "By tomorrow at this time, we'll be home laughing about this whole deal over a couple of cold ones."

Ferrari pulled into the slot in front of number 146 and killed the engine. "Hey, lookit," he said. "What's that damn cart doin' in front of our place?"

"Let's find out," Vic said as he got out of the car. The maid's supply wagon was sitting in front of their door, but no maid was in sight.

He turned to Tony and put a finger to his lips, then got out his key and slowly walked up to the door. His ear to the wood he listened intently. He heard Rocco counting inside, and rolled his eyes in Ferrari's direction.

The key fit easily into the lock, the door opening as he turned it. Rocco, dressed in Jockey shorts, had just finished doing push-ups and was standing before a petite Hispanic maid, posing.

"Get a load of this," Rocco said, flexing his arms above his head. "You ever seen muscles like these?"

"No, *señor*," the woman said nervously.

"How about this?" Rocco turned his back to her and pulled his arms in front of him, rippling his back musculature. "Ain't they the best muscles you ever seen?"

"*Sí, señor*. The best."

"Hey, Roc," D'matto said. "What's going on here anyway?"

"I was just showin' the lady my muscles, that's all," Rocco answered. The woman took the opportunity to hurry past D'matto toward the door. "Nothin' wrong with that."

D'matto grabbed the woman by the arm as she went past. Reaching into his pocket, he pulled a fifty-dollar bill and stuffed it in the front apron pocket of her starched white uniform. "You didn't see anything," he told her, pointing to his lips. "You won't say anything about us."

The woman's dark eyes were frightened as she pulled away from D'matto. "No, *señor*. No. Excuse me, *por favor*. Excuse me."

She hurried out, and Ferrari closed the door behind her.

"What am I gonna do with you, Roc?" D'matto asked in exasperation. "Your pop sent us out here to look after you, and as soon as we turn our back, you're putting it out for some broad who doesn't even speak good English."

"Aw, I didn't do no harm," Rocco said, sitting on the bed.

"What do you mean, no harm?" Vic groaned. "You're running around in your goddamn underwear, and that broad doesn't know what's going on. What if she started screaming?"

Rocco waved off his concern and began to put on his pants. "You're worse than some old woman," he said. "I didn't mean no harm."

"All right." Vic gave him a light slap on the back. "All forgotten."

Rocco stood and zipped up his pants. "Did you get the stuff?"

"Yeah," D'matto said, hefting the heavy suitcase up on the bed and snapping it open. "They may be hayseeds in this lousy town, but they sure do like their guns." He turned the suitcase upside down on the bed, dumping three Ingram MAC-10s and a number of fully loaded clips onto the mattress. "If these don't take care of Joey Giancarlo, the bastard's Superman."

Rocco's eyes lit up like a kid's at Christmas as he picked up one of the miniautomatics and held it out, tracking an invisible assailant across the room. "We can kick up some hell with one of these. When do we do it?"

"Tonight looks good," D'matto answered. "Tony and I drove past Old Sam's place earlier. Practically the whole neighborhood's deserted. It'll be easy in and easy out. A piece of cake."

"Yeah," Rocco grinned. "Well, I got the itch for it. Every night in that stinkin' cell I thought about Old Sam and what I'd do to him when I got out. I just wish Pop had told me more about it."

"Probably nothin' to tell," Ferrari said too quickly.

Rocco looked at him for a long moment. "I ain't that dumb, Tony," he said. "If there was nothin' to tell, he woulda told me. He was holdin' somethin' back and I can't figger out why."

"Don't worry about it," D'matto said. "We've all got our jobs to do. Ben Villani...he's a smart old bastard. He knows what he's doing."

Rocco tracked the empty gun to D'matto, stopping with it pointed to the man's head. He dropped the hammer to click loudly on the empty chamber. "Sure, Vic," he said quietly. "Whatever you say."

"THAT THE SMALLEST YOU GOT?" the clerk at the convenience store asked Bolan as he dropped the twenty-dollar bill and the small plastic container of aspirin tablets on the countertop.

"Yeah." Bolan leaned his head back and massaged his neck muscles. "Sorry."

"Everybody's the same," the man said, ringing up the sale and setting the twenty on top of the drawer as he made the change. "They pay for everything with twenties, then run us out of smaller bills when we really need them."

Bolan glanced down at the stack of Oklahoma City papers on the counter. The lead story was another report on the growing problem of stolen automobiles, adding official speculation to the accounts that the increase could be the result of a theft ring that had recently moved into the area. There were still no leads in the case. Bolan picked up a paper. "Take this out of it, too."

The man glared at him, sorting through the change until he'd paid for the paper, then slamming the cash register drawer shut. "Have a nice day," he said venomously.

"Same to you." Bolan picked up his aspirin and wandered back out to the rented Cougar he and Meredith had picked up at the airport. He paused for a moment to admire the spectacular Oklahoma sunset that streaked the cerulean sky. The weather had turned cool here, but it was nothing like the cold of Colorado. He was comfortable in his sport jacket.

He opened the door on the passenger side. "How about you driving? I want to rest my eyes for a few minutes."

"Sure," Joan said, moving around to the driver's side as Bolan slid into her vacated spot. He glanced at the paper for a second before tossing it into the back seat.

Instead of the jeans and sweatshirts she usually wore on tough assignments, Meredith was wearing a simple print dress that was very becoming. Bolan wondered if the change had anything to do with the fact that she'd heard him talk about Angela Giancarlo and didn't want to walk into a situation with the woman on less than equal terms. Interesting.

"Which way?" she asked as she backed out of the parking slot, a pickup truck hurrying to take her place.

"South," Bolan said. He was fighting with the box of headache pills to get it open. "We're only a couple miles from their neighborhood."

The box came open with a jerk, spilling its contents all over Bolan and the floor and the seats. He closed his eyes and took a deep breath, then calmly picked up the pills and put them back in the package, keeping out three for himself.

"Do you have anything to take those with?" she asked as she pulled into the southbound lane of Western Avenue, passing a line of tract housing and cheap apartments.

He shook his head. "I'll just chew 'em." He popped the pills into his mouth, biting down. The bitter taste was a jaw clencher, but he didn't mind. He felt like punishing himself.

Meredith shook her head and looked at him. "I've never seen you like this before."

Bolan laid his head back on the seat. "I haven't had a headache in twenty years," he said. "Not one."

"Why now?"

"Tension, I think. You don't know what we're getting ready to walk into."

"You're not real fond of the Giancarlos," she commented with a half smile.

"I feel like I'm protecting Lucifer, himself...take a right here." He closed his eyes, massaging his neck again, a little of the tension beginning to drain out of him. "For years I've honed myself to a fine edge when it comes to slime like Old Sam. I'm of two minds whether I'm really serving the people of this country by keeping him alive. It doesn't add up. Good simply can't come out of so much bad."

"But he is helping law enforcement a great deal," she replied. "Already his depositions have resulted in hundreds of indictments."

"I've heard all that before. It doesn't make my headache go away. I knew I was risking just this kind of compromise when I let Hal bring me out of hiding. Now it's all coming home to roost."

"If you don't like it," she told him, "just take a walk. You've done plenty, Mack. Nobody's going to fault you if you beg off now."

"I can't," he said. "That's just the trouble. I've wanted to bolt and run fifty times since we left Denver, but the damn thing keeps dragging me back. I've got to put it all together. One trouble with the world today is that nobody's willing to follow through with what they start. I'm not going to walk out on this one. Two of my people were butchered up in Seattle. I'm going to make sure they didn't die for nothing."

"How's your headache?"

"Better," he said. "Turn left here. After I have a talk with Old Sam, it'll be better still."

"You think he's involved in this himself?" she asked.

"Let me tell you something." He watched the street signs as they drove through the neighborhood. "The old men who run the families, they've got nothing else to do but sit and plot. That's their game: sit and plot. They watch everything around them with eagle eyes, protecting their territory, protecting their position. If someone gets too smart or comes along too fast in the organization, he's removed permanently. Organized crime isn't a democracy, it's a brutal, feudal society. At the heart of its operation is the cruelty of its leaders. The fact that Old Sam has been family head for so long tells you all you need to know about his conniving viciousness. Certainly he's *capable* of being mixed up in this. The son of a bitch is capable of anything."

She turned and looked at him, her face tense. "This really means a lot to you, doesn't it?"

"Crime tends to be the business that brings law breakers and law enforcers together," he answered, beginning to feel a lot better now that he was getting his feelings out. "The victims simply become the tools of the trade. In a lot of ways, the good guys and bad guys are simply different sides of the same coin. Each

exists to complement the other—just business. The
heart goes. The anger goes. Well, lady, the anger never
goes with me. Crime isn't a business to me, it's the
darkness trying to extinguish the light of civilization.
And I've dedicated my life to doing what I can to stop
it. It's my reason for breathing, which is why I don't
mind living out of a suitcase. A home would be a bur-
den to me—just somewhere they could catch me sitting down."

They drove in silence for a while. Joan had never
before heard Bolan speak with such passionate conviction. She didn't know what to say in response. Then
Bolan pointed out where to turn into Giancarlo's
street.

Joan noticed the vacant houses as they drove along.
She looked at Bolan quizzically.

"I know," he said. "Tough to defend."

"What kind of reception are we going to get?" she
asked, pulling into the driveway.

"Figure it out," he said. "We hate each other. They
know how I feel about them, and I've punched out
Joey. There's no love lost one way or the other."

"Not even with Angela?" she asked. She looked
over at him as she stopped the car.

He returned her knowing gaze with his inscrutable
one. "Jury's still out on her," he said. "She didn't ask
to be born."

"Right." Meredith opened her door, getting out and
bringing a large purse with her. Bolan climbed out on
the other side.

As they approached the front door Bolan tensed, not knowing what to expect. The windows and doors were still boarded up from the last time he'd been here. "Hold on to your hat. The road's going to get rough."

They stepped up on the threshold. The door opened, and there stood Joey Giancarlo, looking at them. He was wearing a suit, and had a large adhesive bandage on his right temple, where Bolan had hit him.

Joey grinned and opened the screen door for them. "Belasko!" He sounded delighted. "Good to see you!"

Meredith shared a look with Bolan. "Can I let go of my hat now?" she asked.

He shrugged and followed her into the house.

Joan noticed it seemed a comfortable place, not overpowering like Ottoni's. Just to the left of the front door, were stairs to the second floor. A small hallway led into a den. On the right of the entrance were formal living and dining rooms. The kitchen was at the back of the house.

Joey escorted them back toward the den, speaking over his shoulder as he walked. "You really handled those punks up in Denver. I heard there were lots of them. Guess you really made me take back what I said about you guys."

"Ottoni's dead, though," Bolan returned.

Joey waved a dismissing hand. "Stinking mouthpiece," he said. "Never had an ounce of guts." He turned and gave Meredith the once-over. "Quite a partner you've got yourself this time, Belasko. You must have got a promotion.''

"This is Joan Meredith," Bolan said. Addressing Joan, he nodded in Joey's direction. "Joseph Giancarlo, the essence of subtlety."

"Charmed," she said, holding back a grin.

"Yeah," said Joey. "I'm charmed, too."

They walked into a comfortable den, where Old Sam was sitting in a conversation pit in his stocking feet, watching reruns of *The Munsters* on a big screen television.

"Hey, here's the killer boy." He nodded at Bolan. "I see you left the jungle bunny at home this time."

"She's a dish, isn't she?" Joey said.

The old man nodded again, his eyes and his brain sharp. "What happened to your face, little lady?" he asked, pointing to her bandage.

Joan looked him dead in the eye and said, "The son of a bitch who hit me didn't take his ring off first."

The two men laughed. "She's feisty, too," Old Sam said, his eyes drifting back to the TV. "You ever watch this program?" he asked.

"I can't say that I have," Bolan replied, wondering what had become of Angela.

"Real funny," Old Sam said. "It makes me laugh."

"Well finally!" Angela walked into the den. She was dressed in a casual but elegant double-knit pant suit that set off her lush figure. "We've been waiting dinner for you. Hope you like lasagna." She caught sight of Meredith, her eyes narrowing somewhat. "Nobody told me we had company."

Meredith walked up to her and put out a hand. "You must be Angela. I'm Joan Meredith, Mike's partner."

"Nice work if you can get it," Angela returned, shaking Joan's hand lightly. "Let's eat."

"I don't think—" Bolan began.

Meredith cut him off. "Sounds great to me," she said.

"Good," Angela said. "This is a special celebration tonight to thank Mike Belasko for taking care of our...problem without it spilling over into our lives here."

"Well, it may not be over yet," Bolan replied. "We still don't know—"

"Aw, loosen up," Joey said, leading them into the dining room. "You knocked the stuffing out of them."

They sat down around a large table, elegantly set with fine china and gleaming flatware. There was even a centerpiece of late roses from Old Sam's garden. And food. There was enough food to feed the city police force.

Angela had sat next to Bolan, and kept smiling enigmatically at him. As she passed him the serving bowls, she found many excuses to touch him, attentions that took his mind off his dislike of the Giancarlo men.

The old man picked up one of several bottles of Chianti and passed it to Bolan. "Wine?" he asked.

The big man just passed the bottle to Angela. "We're on duty," he explained.

"Whatdya mean?" Joey asked. "What can possibly happen? You offed the bastards, right?"

"Can't we be a little more civil?" Angela asked.

"Aw," Joey grunted, making a throwaway gesture.

"I'm interested, Mr. Killer," Old Sam said through a mouthful of hot bread. "So you don't think our worries are over?"

"Far from it," Bolan said. "There's no reason to suspect that they are."

"Wait a minute," Joey countered. "From what your boss told us on the phone, all the people who were after us got killed in Denver. Isn't that true?"

"Sure it's true," Bolan said. "I'm sure we got everybody who was on to you . . . except one."

"Who's that?" the old man asked.

Bolan used the edge of his fork to cut into the lasagna. He took a bit—spicy hot, Sicilian. "Whoever it was who hired them. I found a bag full of nearly half a million dollars in cash in the trunk of the killers' car. Somebody paid them, and that somebody is still out there."

"I heard there was a hit list, too," Old Sam said.

"Right," Bolan said. "And your name wasn't on it."

"Doesn't that explain it, then?" Angela asked. "Wherever the information came from, they weren't able to get my father's address."

"We all know where it came from." Joey stuffed his mouth with salad. "Ben Villani hired those punks, that son of a bitch."

"It doesn't add up," Bolan said, turning his attention to Old Sam. "First of all, the leak in Justice had the same access to your names as he did to the others. So it doesn't make sense for him to take the little fish and let the big fish go. Second, do you really think that Ben Villani would hire mercenaries out of a magazine to do his dirty work?"

"Whatever happened to the Justice Department leak?" Angela asked.

"What happened to him is that they let him get away," Joey said. "Government people always look out for their own, right?"

Bolan ignored him and turned to Old Sam. "What do you think?"

"I think I'm tired of all this," the man said sadly. "I don't think about these things no more. I just want to live out my last days in peace . . . surrounded by the love of my family."

"You're going to have to think about it," Meredith said. "Because if we're right, they'll be here to get you, maybe tonight."

"So, what happens, happens," Old Sam said.

"What are you getting my father all upset about?" Joey asked. "It's all over, you know? Soon they'll take

Ben Villani away to jail for good, and it'll all just be spit in the wind. They took their shot. They blew it. End of story."

Bolan turned to the old man once more. "Ben Villani didn't hire those goons and you know it. He'd use someone from the family. This is vendetta."

"No!" Old Sam said loudly, slamming a hand down hard on the table. "The vendetta is finished. I'm all through with that life."

"You can never get free of it," Bolan told him. "You should know that better than anyone. You marry it, live with it, die with it, but you never walk away. Did you ever let anyone walk away?"

"Stop it!" Old Sam shouted. "You're just trying to make me upset because you're jealous of my life here and my family. You're just a killer, you got nothin'. You don't know the feelin' of the love and respect of your children. The family, the blood...that's all that means anything. Everything I did in my life was for my wife, God rest her soul, and my family, and I'm gonna enjoy them now."

"You can't walk away from your past," Bolan said.

"Enough." Angela's eyes pleaded with Bolan. "Leave my father alone now, please. He can't answer your questions."

Bolan looked around the table. Everyone, including Joanie, was staring at him. He picked his napkin off his lap and wiped his mouth. "I think I'd better do a brief check of the neighborhood," he said. "Just to make sure."

"How long does this go on?" Joey asked. "When do you leave us alone? You know, we got a business to run here, a life. We can't be hidin' out forever because of your cockamamy notions."

Bolan stood. "Yeah, I read about your 'business' in today's papers."

"What's that supposed to mean?"

"Nothing." Bolan winked at him, then he looked at Meredith. "When you're through eating, I want you checking the perimeter and the house defenses."

She nodded. "Sure."

"I'll be back." He started out of the room.

"I'm going with you," Angela said, standing to follow him.

Bolan thought about trying to stop her, but figured any such attempt would have about as much effect as anything he said to the Giancarlos. They were going to live their lives as they chose, no matter what. Who was he to tell them otherwise?

He moved outside, glad for the fresh air. Old Sam rankled him like a festering sore. It made him feel sick, diseased, just to be around him.

Now that the sun was completely down it was cooler, but it still felt good to be outside. A strong breeze was wafting up from the Gulf of Mexico, and he turned up his collar to head into it.

"Chilly," Angela said from beside him. She was hugging her arms around her chest.

"Don't you want to go in and get a coat?" he asked.

She shook her head. "I'm fine this way. Where are we going?"

"I figured we'd go down the right side of the street to the corner, checking houses, then come back up on the other side."

They started across the lawn to a long, brick ranch-style house with a three-car garage next door.

"What about the back of our house?"

"You have neighbors and dogs and fences behind you," he answered. "They'll come in this way. Even with us watching, it's their best shot."

"Do you really think people will be coming here looking for my father?" she asked in a tiny voice that made him realize for the first time that she was frightened.

"It didn't end last night," he said. "Your father knows it, too. Apparently he's just tired of everything. Which brings me to my next point: when we get back to the house, I want you to get in your car and go back to your motel."

She looked up at him, ready to protest, but thought better of it when she saw the look he was giving her. "Okay. I know better than to argue with you."

"Good girl."

"Can I ask you a question straight out?" They had reached the back of the first house, and Bolan was trying the doors and looking at the curtainless windows for any signs of forced entry.

"Sure," he said.

"Is there anything between you and the woman?"

He smiled down at her. "Just business," he said.

She grinned. "Good." Then she leaned against him, his arm quite naturally going around her shoulder. "That's better... warmer."

They did a complete turn around the property, then went on to the next house, a two-story building whose second-floor windows were designed to look like huge gas lanterns.

"Are any of these houses occupied?" he asked as they walked around the place checking doors and windows.

She pointed to another ranch-style house across the street. "I think that one is, but the people are away on vacation."

They moved to the next house. There were three on each side of the cul-de-sac that ended at the Giancarlo house. On the far side of the street that ran past Willow Way was a creek and small park.

They walked mostly in silence, Bolan enjoying the closeness even as he kept a wary, professional eye on the territory. The incongruity of this quiet moment spent with the offspring of a man he considered the closest thing to the devil was not lost on him. He simply chose not to dwell on it. He chose simply to enjoy. Rays of sunshine fell too seldom in the Executioner's driven life.

When they finished their rounds of the last house on the block, Bolan reluctantly broke from the woman. She waited on the corner while he crossed close to Willow Way. It seemed logical to him that if anyone were coming to commit murder, they wouldn't want to jog two miles to the getaway car.

The streets were clear in all directions, the night quiet except for a dog barking somewhere, its wail plaintive and distant.

Angela met him at the first house on the other side of Willow Way. When he didn't make a move to put his arm around her again, she moved up close and did it for him.

"When do you go back to Hollywood?" he asked as he peered in the window of a garage door.

"Tomorrow...or the next day," she said. "As soon as something breaks with this."

"I wish you'd go soon," he said. "I worry about you here."

She slapped him on the arm. "Trying to get rid of me?"

"No way. I'm just concerned."

They strolled aorund to the patio door and peered inside. The house was dark, empty.

"I guess we won't have much time together," she said. "Our lives are so..."

"Different," he finished. "No. We won't."

She stopped walking, drawing him close to her as she leaned against the brick wall of the house. "Maybe we need to make the best of what we do have," she said in a low voice. Then she pulled his face down to hers, kissing him deeply.

She fit easily into his arms, her body molding to his. In the chill of the evening, her body was hot fire on the ice that was his psyche.

"Oh, Mike," she whispered in his ear when he reluctantly broke the kiss.

He took a breath, his body tense, and he knew he had to get his mind back on business. "We'd better get moving."

"No," she protested, trying to pull him back. "You can't leave me like this." She wrapped herself around him, caressing, making small sounds down deep in her throat, driving him crazy. "Take me here," she whispered in a throaty voice. "Please."

He pushed her away. "Not here," he said. "Not now."

"Why not? There may not be a later, Mike. Make love to me now, before it's too late."

"I can't," he said firmly. "We'll both just have to deal with that as it is. If there's no later, then maybe it just isn't meant to happen." He put his arm out to her. "Come on, let's finish up."

Her eyes flashed angrily. "No," she said. "I'm too embarrassed." With that, she burst into tears and ran off.

He almost went after her, but to what end? It wouldn't change the way things were. It would only confuse them more.

A weight on his spirits, he continued checking the houses, arriving back at the Giancarlos' ten minutes later. Joan Meredith was sitting on the trunk of the

Cougar waiting for him when he got back, her big purse slung around her shoulder.

"Lovers' quarrel?" she asked.

"Don't be catty, Joan. It doesn't suit you. Everything secure?"

She nodded. "You sure you're right about all this? It seems so quiet here, so remote from trouble of any kind."

"People can convince themselves of all sorts of things," he said. "But that won't change the facts, and the facts on this one stink."

"Yeah," she said. "By the way, I'm sorry about what I said before."

He waved it off. "I probably deserved it."

She jumped off the car. "I checked in with Hal a few minutes ago," she said, dusting off the back of her dress. "Rocco Villani's broken out of Joliet."

Bolan shook his head. "There's a man who didn't know when he had it good."

"Do you think there's any connection?" she asked. "The timing certainly is..."

"Auspicious," he finished, and nodded grimly. "I think things are coming to a head. For once we're positioned perfectly. Let's go back in."

"Sure," she said, but he could tell there was something else on her mind. Finally she said, "Do you mind if I ask you another question?"

"Shoot."

They walked toward the front door, the boarded-up windows making the place look dilapidated. "*Is* there anything going on between you and Angela?"

He laughed. "That's the same thing she asked me about you." She waited for him to say something more, but he left it at that.

"There's only one thing about her that doesn't make sense to me," Meredith continued, undaunted. "Why would a woman with such lovely hair cover it up with a wig?"

"What do you mean?" he said.

She smiled. "Men are all alike. You really haven't noticed, have you?"

He shook his head.

"Angela Giancarlo uses a black wig to cover a head of blond hair. Maybe she just needed to wash it."

"Blond hair," Bolan said, and looked at the house. "Blond hair."

12

Where were all the people? Where? Chasen drove through the neighborhood, surprised so many houses were dark and empty—like in a ghost town. Oklahoma City. He had no idea of how he'd even made it this far. His day had been a nightmare of diminishing returns and memory lapses, huge chunks of reality slipping away from him as he used every ounce of his brain to stay on the road and head in the right direction.

The wound in his side was a huge gash of agony that nothing could touch; not even the last of the coke could deaden the pain. His head swam in confusion, even the simplest of concepts difficult to dwell upon. He sweated continuously, and his eyes played tricks on him in the dark.

He realized his body was screaming for rest, a rest his brain denied him. He had to keep moving, to reach this place, this outpost where he was sure, *sure* that he would be taken care of. It was that thought that kept him going, that dream that pushed sleep and sanity aside. If he could only reach this place, everything would be all right.

He had no idea of how it would be all right, or why, or how he'd accomplish it. Those were concerns of the moment, and the moment could not arrive until he reached his destination—this ghost town where the empty houses held large, cavernous eyes that watched him pass, and the naked trees swayed angrily in the high wind, their branches reaching out to him, trying to take him into their horrid dark embrace.

He concentrated, trying to bring back the address, an address that had escaped him many times during the course of his cross-country odyssey. He drove past houses on one side, a darkness of trees on the other. Then he saw it, the name on the street, standing out in bright contrast under the harsh glare of the street-light. Somewhere back in the seething maelstrom that his brain had become, the idea popped up that the light was God's hand directing him to his salvation.

He jerked the wheel hard, the Toyota careening to the left, up over the curb and down a long embankment. He saw the darkness rush up at him and rode it down in horror, unable to do anything to stop his headlong plunge.

The car bottomed out hard, hitting ground at a forty-five-degree angle. The force threw him up over the steering wheel into the windshield, which he cracked with his head, smashing it into a crazed spiderweb.

He might have passed out, he wasn't sure, was never sure of anything anymore. He found himself crumpled against the wheel, the car tilted crazily, his mind tilting even more. Somehow he had the sense to reach for the door handle and press it down, the door swinging open, tumbling him out into shallow water.

He lay on his back in soggy leaves, a small creek running around and over him. When he opened his eyes, he saw he was surrounded by branches, all of them reaching, trying to grab him.

It would have been so nice, so peaceful, just to lie there and let the branches have their way. The fight was becoming so difficult. How had all this started? How did he get here? There was something... something he had to do before he could rest.

Slowly he rolled over. The creek water was cold on his face, and tasted of mud and leaf mulch. On hands and knees he began crawling back up the embankment.

Something was getting into his eyes, stinging. He wiped at them and found blood running from a gash on his head.

The climb seemed interminable, the hillside steep and treacherous. Several time he lost his balance and slid partway back down before finally making it to the roadway at the top. On level ground again, he stood on shaky legs. He was so weak. It was all he could do to power himself.

He managed to cross the street and stood there for a moment, bathed in the God-given radiance of the streetlight, gazing up at the signpost. Willow Way. His salvation.

He stared down the cul-de-sac, at the only house on the whole block that had lights on. It was time for decisions. What should he do now that he was here? He tried to think, to plan, but it was too difficult. He finally decided to wait for Yvette and her friends. They'd be glad to see him. He was sure Yvette would have explained everything to them by now and that she was sorry for shooting him.

Across the street was a house with windows that looked like lanterns instead of staring eyes. That would be a good place to wait, warm and inviting. When Yvette and her friends came to this place, he'd surprise them and they'd be glad to see him.

He crossed the street, his legs numb and weak. He had no control over his movements, falling several times and weaving drunkenly before making it to the house. He tried the front door but it was locked. Around the back, he found a stick and used it to break a window in the back door, reaching through to unlock the place and let himself in.

The house was dark and empty and quiet, like a huge tomb. What moonlight there was filtered stark, angular shadows into the empty, morguelike rooms. It frightened and depressed him to be in this place, the house of the dead.

Suddenly dizziness swept over him. He tried to lean against a wall for support, but slid down instead, ending up in a heap on the floor. Too spent to do anything else, he buried his face in hands and began to cry.

BOLAN SAT WATCHING the Giancarlos in their den, while Meredith stood her watch at the window of one of the second-floor bedrooms. The old man sat like a statue in front of the television, which was never turned off. A silent telephone sat next to him on an end table. He never moved; he never laughed; he never reacted. Bolan sometimes wondered if he was even alive or if he was simply a festering ball of meanness in human form. Joey paced nervously through the house, unable to sit still for any period of time. The genial mood he'd been in when greeting Bolan at the door had now left him, replaced by a kind of unpleasant morose sullenness. Bolan could make no sense of it. Angela had still not left for the motel, using the dinner dishes as an excuse to hang around far longer than she should have.

He had cornered her alone in the kitchen earlier and asked her about her blond hair. She'd told him it was a dye job, that her natural color was black. She wore the wig so her father wouldn't see what she'd done and get angry. Old Sam had always called bleached blondes "floozies." Bolan wasn't sure if he accepted that explanation, but it would do until something better came along.

The news about Rocco was interesting. He was beginning to develop a theory about what was happening here, and Rocco fit very nicely into the picture. He expected they'd be seeing the man, if not tonight, then soon. Very soon.

"Mike!" Meredith called from upstairs.

He jumped up and hurried through the house, taking the stairs two at a time until he joined her. She sat in a chair by the window in the darkened guest room, her face set in perplexity as she turned to him.

"Take a look," she said. "I have no idea."

He looked out the window in the direction of her pointing finger. A man was trying to cross the street. He was obviously in great difficulty, either drunk or hurt. He kept falling, then slowly picking himself up and staggering a few more feet before falling again. They watched, fascinated, as he finally made his way across the road and a lawn, and started trying to open the front door of one of the vacant houses.

"What do you make of it?" she asked.

"Could be a vagrant," he said. "Could be a sacrificial lamb."

The man moved out of sight around the back of the house. Seconds later they heard a distant shattering of glass.

"What do we do?" Meredith asked.

"We go get him and ask him what he wants."

She smiled. "Actually, I was getting tired of just hanging around anyway."

They hurried downstairs, Angela meeting them by the door. "What is it?" she asked.

"Probably nothing," Bolan asked. "We think a vagrant just broke into one of the houses down the block. We're going to check it out."

Her eyes narrowed in concern and she laid a gentle hand on his arm. "Be careful," she said.

He nodded curtly, then opened the front door, peering up and down the block before slipping silently into the shrubbery next to the door, Meredith right behind him.

Big Thunder was out of his harness and in his hands, a live shell in the chamber. Meredith had dug a .45 out of her big purse and held it, barrel skyward, the safety catch off and ready.

"We edge the houses," he explained, applying the same rules to the urban jungle that he'd used in Nam. "Keep to the shadows. Stay low. We'll go in the same way he did, through the back."

She nodded. "Whenever you're ready."

"Now." In a semicrouch he charged through the bushes and around the side of the house, following the fence line to the property next door. He crossed that backyard staying close to the vacant house, his movements not visible from the target residence.

He reached the edge of the house, taking a quick look at the one next door that was their target, making sure no one was watching from the windows. He turned to Meredith, who had just moved up beside him, breathing heavily. "Here we go," he said, and raced across the space between the houses, coming up on the back door with its window broken.

The door stood wide open, swinging slowly in and out on the Oklahoma wind. Bolan put his back to the wall and edged around the doorframe, peering in. He was looking at a laundry room. An archway led into the rest of the house.

He entered the house slowly, with measured steps, Meredith duplicating his moves. When he reached the archway, he stuck his head through. The kitchen was to the left, the living room to the right. Turning to Meredith, he pointed at her, then pointed to the right. Then he indicated that he'd be moving to the left.

She nodded. They both moved silently through the archway at the same time.

Bolan turned left, hitting the empty kitchen, from which another archway opened into a large dining room. From somewhere in there he could hear sounds, whimpering sounds. He held out Big Thunder two-handed in front of him.

He took a long breath, trying to identify the exact location of the noises, then dived through the opening, rolling, coming up with the AutoMag extended to arms' length.

A man lay crumpled on the floor, crying. He was covered with filth and blood, looking near death. A movement to Bolan's left caught his eye. He swung around and saw Joan coming through an entry in a crouch, her .45 pointed at the man, too.

They shared a look. Bolan shrugged. "Keep your hands where we can see them," he addressed the man, who slowly looked up at them.

"Are you the ones who can save me?" he asked. "Oh, please, I can help you. I know... I know... so... much."

He fell back, weak, Bolan moving up to him and patting him down for identification. He had none.

Meredith joined Bolan as he pulled a penlight out of the webbing and played its light over the man.

"Maybe a bum who got beat up pretty bad," the woman said, looking at the blood-soaked shirt tied around his middle.

"I don't think so," Bolan said. "Look at his shoes...they're expensive. And that's a twenty-dollar haircut if I've ever seen one."

"Then who the hell is he?"

"I don't know," he replied. "Let's get him over to the house and call an ambulance from there. He may not last it much longer."

"It's odd," Meredith said, "but there's something...I don't know, familiar about this guy."

Bolan leaned down close to the man, who stared back at him through glazed, half-closed eyes. "Who are you?" he asked.

"It wasn't my fault," the man mumbled. He was incoherent, babbling.

"We're going to get you to your feet," Bolan said, "and get you some help."

"Help," the man repeated. "Yes, help."

Bolan put the stranger's arm around his shoulder, and wrapped his own arm around the man, grabbing his belt to avoid pressure on the injury to his side. Bolan stood, the other man leaning on him heavily.

"We'll go back the way we came," he said.

"You want me to take a side?" Joan asked.

Bolan shook his head. "You take point. We want to make sure this isn't some kind of setup."

He half walked, half dragged the deranged man to the back door, Meredith going ahead to keep watch. Their progress was slow and they made good targets, with Joan hurrying to each secure point, then waving them over.

When they reached the Giancarlo house, Bolan picked the man up and carried him across the threshold, taking him right back to the den.

"What the hell you got there?" Old Sam asked angrily. "You're not gonna put that mess on my good furniture."

Bolan just glared at him and laid the stranger on a love seat that matched Old Sam's couch.

"You're gonna pay for cleanin' that," Old Sam said, then went back to watching television.

Angela moved up close, her eyes narrowed as she studied the man. Joey was nowhere to be seen.

The man's eyes suddenly fluttered and opened wide. Angela took a step back when he looked at her.

"Thank God," he whispered. "Yvette." Then his eyes closed and he sighed deeply with satisfaction.

Bolan straightened slowly, then turned to look at the woman. "So, that's it," he said in disbelief.

"What do you mean?" she asked, turning away so the man on the couch wouldn't see her if he opened his eyes.

"What's going on?" Meredith asked, puzzled.

Bolan pointed to the man on the couch. "Meet Ken Chasen," he told her. He walked over to Angela, who stared at him defiantly, and jerked the wig off her head, her blond hair falling free. "And his contact, Yvette."

"You don't know what you're talking about," Angela said.

Bolan walked over to stare down at Old Sam. "You figured it out before I did. I'll bet this is really sticking in your craw."

"I don't understand," Meredith said.

Bolan swung around and looked hard at Angela. "You're good, lady. You're real good. You even had me going for a while. I can just picture you laying on the charm with that poor son of a bitch lying over there. 'Oh Ken, I need you. Please make love to me. Take me now.' I'm telling you, Angela, you're really professional."

"Writing wasn't all I did in Hollywood," she announced proudly. "But when my father turned government stooge, he lost his power out there and I got shelved."

"I want you clowns to put your hands behind your heads," Joey said from the doorway, leveling a Remington pump shotgun at Bolan.

"Ah," Bolan responded. "The gang's all here."

"Just do what I said," Joey said.

"Sure," Bolan replied. He nodded compliance to Meredith. "The fact is, I wouldn't miss this little show for the world."

"What little show?" Angela asked.

"Unless I miss my guess," Bolan went on, interlocking his fingers behind his head, "you'll be having some visitors in a little while."

"What—"

"Never mind, Angela, he's just bullshitting." Joey motioned with the barrel of the gun for Bolan and Meredith to move closer together. "Get their guns, sis."

Angela, who looked stunning as a blonde, felt inside Bolan's jacket to the combat webbing.

"What in the *hell* is going on here?" Meredith asked as Angela took the .45 out of her hand. She was still thoroughly confused.

"It's unbelievably simple," Bolan explained. "Joey is our mystery man, the man who hired Burnett and his scum to do the people in hiding, using his darling sister, Angela, to set up this poor so-and-so." Bolan looked over at Old Sam, who still sat calmly on the sofa. "How about it, Sam? Some kids you've got."

"But why?" Meredith asked.

"I don't have all the answers," Bolan replied, sitting on the arm of the love seat, "but I've got a pretty good idea. Let's say that Joey goes to Ben Villani and offers him a deal: the lives of the protected witnesses in exchange for Villani's territory. What an interesting way for a young man to gain himself a foothold in the world. Must be in the blood."

"But Old Sam wasn't on the hit list," Meredith said.

"That's right," Bolan returned. "Can I put my hands down?"

"No," Joey said.

Bolan shrugged. "Okay. That point about the hit list screwed me up for a while, too," he went on. "But then it made perfect sense. He can pay the hit man with money glommed from his chop shops here in town. He fixes it so the others are killed first. That way, if it works, he can do Old Sam himself. If it doesn't work, he simply leaves things as they are and hasn't lost his meal ticket. Villani isn't any the wiser because he never knew the addresses, and things continue as they were."

"Pretty smart, huh?" Joey bragged.

"To a point." Bolan looked at Old Sam. "What do you think of your loving family now?"

The old man sat silent, face expressionless.

"Joey was glad to see us when we showed up tonight," Bolan said. "Hell, why not? We'd tied up all his loose ends for him. All he had to do was blow away his old man, then head to Chicago to take over operations. It would have worked, too."

"Except for him." Meredith pointed at the comatose Ken Chasen. "How did he get here?"

"That I don't know," Bolan answered, "although he's obviously been down some roads. He knew the address because he copied it from the computer file and memorized it. The why of it is beyond me, though I have to think that sweet Angela...pardon me, Yvette, had something to do with it."

"It's still rock solid," Joey boasted. "We just take care of you two, plus my father, and say we were attacked. The rest of the plan still stands."

"Funny you should mention rocks," Bolan said, his agile mind linking one thought to another. "Your plan is about to run into a small problem. You thought you were too smart. I'll bet you went up and visited Ben Villani in Chicago, didn't you?"

Joey just looked at him, his jaw slackening. Old Sam began to curse, very softly, in Italian.

Joey moved to his father, his hands held out in front of him. "There's nothing personal here," he told the old man with sincerity. "It's just business. That's all."

Old Sam leveled his still powerful eyes on Joey. "I will live to see you in your grave. You and your sister."

Bolan looked at the old man, then back at his son. "Well, I don't know how, but they traced you back here when you left, probably because you got cocky and didn't pay attention." Joey jerked around to face him. "What, you think Villani doesn't take his vendetta seriously? He's used you, Joey. Yesterday morning he sprang Rocco from Joliet. He probably waited until tonight to hit you because he wanted to make sure Ottoni was hit before tidying up. Really neat, huh, Sam?"

The old man looked at him this time, and the darkness in his eyes was a frightening thing. Still he didn't move. Still he didn't talk. He simply sat and exuded the evil that had infected his entire family. Animals, all of them animals, Bolan thought, living on the ragged edge of death and deceit.

VIC D'MATTO PULLED the Lincoln up about half a block from the intersection of Willow Way. The dark neighborhood was the perfect locale. With any luck they'd be on their charter flight out of this hick town within an hour and a half. Rocco sat beside him in the front seat with the shooters, Tony in the back.

He turned the car off and twisted to look at Rocco. "I figure we go up on both sides of the street and use the empty houses as cover."

"Sounds fine," Rocco said, pulling out one of the Ingrams and jamming a magazine into the breech. "But first, we got somethin' to talk over."

D'matto looked at his watch. "Maybe we ought to do the hit first, kid, and talk later."

Rocco gave a half smile, then reached out a beefy hand, grabbing Vic by the lapels and jamming the gun into his face. "I say we talk now."

"Roc...come on." D'matto was more angry than fearful. "We haven't got time for games here."

"This ain't no game, Vic," he said, eyes shining in the darkness. "You're gonna tell me how you found out about this place, and you're gonna tell me quick."

D'matto looked into his face and saw that he meant what he said. Vic was caught in the fire, because if he told, Ben wouldn't understand the reasons why. "I can't tell you. Your pop would kill me."

"And I'll kill you if you don't," Rocco said.

"Tony," D'matto said. "Get this son of a bitch off me!"

Ferrari began to stir in the back seat.

"I want you to do some thinking before you move, Tony," Rocco told him, his eyes still locked with D'matto's. "When my old man dies, who're you gonna take orders from—Vic or me? In fact, it's about time for the old man to get out of the way, anyhow. He's gotten weak. He's just pissing away his business."

"Don't listen to him, Tony," D'matto said.

"Okay," Ferrari answered, "but Vic—"

"That's right," Rocco broke in. "When my pop goes, you think I'm gonna keep this old Mustache Pete around, either? You gotta make your choices now, Tony."

"Ain't no choice . . . boss," Ferrari said. "What do you want me to do?"

D'matto saw the power pass from one generation to the next, right in front of him, and knew enough to move with the tide. "Okay, I'll tell ya."

"Go for it," Rocco said.

"Your pop made a deal with Joey Giancarlo to bump off the protected witnesses, so there'd be no evidence against him. He told Joey he'd hand over his territory in exchange. But Joey, he didn't give us the people's addresses, so when he leaves, Tony and I follow him to the airport, right to the gate of a plane going to Oklahoma City. Then we just checked, figuring chop shops would be the place for them to start down here with no competition. We found some legit businesses called Lucky Sam's Body Shops and got the owner's address. This is it.''

"Why didn't my pop tell me all this?" Rocco asked.

"I don't know...maybe he was afraid you wouldn't understand why he made the deal. Hell, Rocco, he did it for you."

"That's crap," Rocco said. "He kept his mouth shut about it because he figured if I got bumped off down here, he could still cut his deal with Joey. What else?"

"Nothing else." D'matto shrugged. "That's all we know."

Rocco grinned. "That's enough then," he said, but kept his grip on D'matto's shirt.

"Let me go, Roc." D'matto was beginning to see the handwriting on the wall.

"I've got a problem with that," Rocco said. "You see, Vic, you told all your secrets. You can't be trusted anymore."

D'matto stared at him, recognizing the moment that he had always known would come, ever since the beginning thirty years ago.

"Tony," Rocco said, "do me a favor."

"Sure, boss," Tony replied.

"Shoot this son of a bitch for me. Then let's go up and get Old Sam and Joey."

Tony leaned over the seat, looking hard at D'matto. D'matto nearly laughed at the thought of stupid Tony being stupid Rocco's right-hand man. He'd just as soon be dead as have to live with something like that.

Tony looked him in the eye. "Nothin' personal," he said matter-of-factly. "I'll tell your sister goodbye."

With that, he brought the MAC-10 up and stuck it in D'matto's face, pulling the trigger. D'matto knew a second of bright red, then quickly ebbing blackness.

ANGELA GIANCARLO had dumped out Joan Meredith's purse on the floor and was sifting through the contents when they heard the gunshot, everyone starting to attention. Bolan pulled his arm away from his head long enough to check his watch.

"Right on time, Joey," he said.

"Maybe it was a car backfire." Angela picked up a pair of handcuffs from the scattered contents of the purse. "Look what I found."

"I wonder how many men Rocco brought with him?" Bolan said idly. "They could surround this place pretty quickly, wouldn't you say so, Joan?"

"Absolutely," Meredith replied, getting into the swing of Bolan's needling. "A couple of guns won't do much good."

Joey was looking around, nervous, as Old Sam continued to sit quietly. "Angie," he said, "come here and keep an eye on them. I'm going to take a look outside."

Angela moved over and took the shotgun from her brother, her face hard as she aimed high. Joey ran to the front door.

"You're good with the baloney," Bolan said to her. "I wonder if you've got the stomach for the killing."

"I shot *him*," she said proudly, pointing the gun barrel at the unconscious Chasen, who was tossing restlessly.

"Yeah," Bolan said, "but how about when *you're* looking down the barrel of somebody else's gun? You got the guts for that?"

She chewed on her lower lip, then looked at her father. "Will you help us out?" she asked.

He stared at her for a second, then went back to watching television.

Joey charged back into the room, agitated. "There's at least two of them," he said, "and they're on both sides of the street."

"What do we do?" Angela asked.

"Yvette!" Chasen called from the couch. "Yvette, where are you?"

"Why don't you make a deal with them?" Bolan said. "What do you think, Sam? Think they can cut a deal?"

"Let's lock these two up first." Joey grabbed Joan's handcuffs.

"Why don't we just kill them?" Angela asked.

"Because," Bolan said, "if you just tie us up, you can use the guns of Rocco and his friend to shoot us with, and take yourselves completely off the hook.

Joey's scenario is coming true—if you can stay alive long enough."

"Shut up!" Joey yelled, getting behind Bolan to push him. "Get in the kitchen."

"Sure, Joey," Bolan said. "Whatever you say. You're the boss, right, Sam?"

They all walked into the kitchen. Joey opened the cabinet doors beneath the sink and bent to look at the water pipes. "Down on the floor," he said.

"Looks pretty dirty down there," Bolan needled him.

"Down on the fucking floor!"

Bolan and Meredith lay down on the floor, Joey making them stretch their hands up to the plumbing.

"Angie," Joey said, taking the shotgun from her. "Get down there and chain 'em around the pipe."

Angela knelt on the floor close to them, reaching under the sink.

"We've got to stop meeting like this," Bolan said. "I'm ready to make love now if you want."

"Stop it!" she screamed. "Would you just stop it!"

"What's wrong?" Bolan asked in concern, working as hard as he could to rattle her. He wanted both of them nervous and as off balance as possible. Confusion was his friend right now. It would cause them to make mistakes.

The woman cuffed Bolan's left arm to Meredith's right, the pipes between them. She stood. "Got it."

"Okay," Joey said. "Grab a gun. They're comin' in." He ran out of the kitchen, Angela behind him.

As soon as they were gone, Bolan looked at Meredith. "Let's see what we can do about getting the hell out of here."

He slid up closer to the sink, getting up to a crouch, listening to Joey and Angela screaming at each other in the distance.

"You see anything?"

"No...no! Where are they?"

"Try upstairs...upstairs!"

Bolan looked into the cabinet, then pulled out a bottle of dishwashing detergent. "Just what the doctor ordered," he said, then reached around the pipes to squirt the liquid soap all over Joan's hand and wrist.

"I washed after dinner," she said.

"Pull for all you're worth," he said, then yelled to the others, "See anything yet? Maybe they're in the back!"

Meredith began working her wrist against the cuffs, pulling, twisting, always exerting pressure.

"I see something!" Angela screamed shrilly from upstairs. Then came the sound of breaking glass and machine gun fire as she opened up with Bolan's AutoMag, blasting out most of the clip on the first burst. She had just effectively taken herself out of the fighting.

"Damn! Damn!" Joey screamed. He opened the front door to push the shotgun through the crack and fire, then pulled it back in.

Return fire began beating against the side of the house. More glass broke and Angela screamed from upstairs.

"It's coming," Meredith whispered. "I'm starting to slide out."

"Quickly," Bolan urged. "We're running out of time."

"You are a cool one."

"Just hurry," he said.

"Yvette!" Chasen called from the next room.

The shotgun went off several more times, fire concentrating on the area of the front door.

"There!" Meredith slipped her wrist free.

"Good girl." Bolan pulled his arm around the pipes and stood, the empty cuff dangling from his wrist. They ran back into the den, where the Beretta and Joan's .45 lay on the couch next to Old Sam. He was still watching television.

There was a groan from the doorway. Joey Giancarlo, blood covering his chest and running freely from his mouth, stumbled into the den without his gun and staggered toward his father.

"I...I..." He was reaching out to Old Sam, his eyelids fluttering. "I..."

The old man wouldn't even look at him. Joey stumbled with a strangled cry and fell dead at his father's feet.

Hearing more noise at the door, both Bolan and Meredith crouched, as two very stupid men charged into their withering cross fire. The first one through was a young, lean man, whom Bolan took high and Meredith took low, the blistering sting of their automatics chopping him up in pieces. Blood squirted from his falling body to cover the walnut-paneled walls.

Rocco Villani was right behind, looking mean. His eyes opened wide in surprise when a burst from the Beretta diced him across the chest, destroying those marvelous pectorals that did nothing to stop the relentless drive of 9 mm death. He went down with a loud shout, his legs sliding out from under him as he crashed against the coffee table in front of Old Sam, then landed beside the body of Joey Giancarlo.

"Check outside!" Bolan said, as he moved up to Rocco to make sure he was dead.

"What about Angela?" Meredith called as she moved out to the hall.

"She didn't take any extra magazines. She probably ran out of ammo in the first minute."

As Meredith moved cautiously to the front door, Bolan stood staring down at Rocco Villani. Old Sam had torn himself away from his TV program and he too, was looking, the barest hint of a smile on his face.

Rocco still drew raspy breath and opened his eyes to look up. "B-Belasko?" he said in confusion.

"The name's Bolan," the Executioner said. "Goodbye." He raised the Beretta and put a round through the man's brain.

"Look what I found," Meredith announced from the hallway. She came in, pushing Angela Giancarlo in front of her. "Nobody else outside."

"S-stop," came Ken Chasen's shaky voice. They all turned to see him holding the Ingram that had dropped from Rocco's hands when he fell. He was awake now, eyes wide, as he pointed the gun at Joan Meredith.

"Ken," Angela said, smiling.

"Let's go... Yvette," Chasen said. He was having trouble holding the gun steady.

"Let me get this gun first." She reached for Meredith's .45.

"No!" Chasen said. "No m-more guns. The last time you... you..."

"Then you kill them," she told him. "Shoot them for me, darling."

His eyes filled with fear, his hands shaking. "L-let's just g-go. N-no killing. I c-can't."

She walked toward him. "Then give me the gun. We've got to take care of..."

"No," he said. "Come... with me."

"Give me the goddamn gun," she shouted, "you slimy wimp! God, how did I ever let you put your sleazy hands on me. I had to go throw up whenever we finished making love. Why can't you be a man?"

"That's n-not true," he said. "You l-love me."

"Coward," she spit, moving closer. "You're nothing but a stinking mama's boy."

He began breathing heavily, terror filling his eyes as she walked up and tried to grab the gun away from him. It went off then, its pop loud, obscene. Angela fell to her knees, blood welling up between the fingers she held over her stomach.

Old Sam watched her, expressionless. She turned to her father, pleading with her eyes, then fell backward to stare, unseeing, at the ceiling.

Bolan took a step toward Chasen, but it was too late. When the man saw Angela on the floor, he began to wail, then brought the MAC-10 up to his temple and pulled the trigger on full auto, splattering himself over the whole room.

Bolan and Meredith exchanged glances. She finally understood what it was about these people that Bolan had known and felt so deeply and for such a long time. As one, they both turned to look at Old Sam.

The man had picked up the phone and was punching up a number. Bolan walked up to stare at him as he waited for his call to go through.

"Yeah," the old man said. "This is Sam Giancarlo. I want to talk with Ben Villani. Yeah . . ." He looked up coldly at Bolan for a second, then returned to the call. "Hello, Ben . . . this is Sam. I just want you to know that I got your boy, he's laying dead at my feet. He's all blasted away, you bastard. I hope you choke on it. I'm gonna fix you good for all this, you see."

He hung up the phone then and looked at Bolan. "You better get your boss on the phone," he said. "It looks like I'm gonna hafta move again."

"That's all you have to say after all this?" Joan asked from across the room.

The man turned and spit on the floor. "Sure. I can tell you to go to hell."

"You're a mad dog who fathered mad dogs," Bolan said. "Only an animal could be so unaffected by the treachery and death of its children."

"So, I'm an animal." Old Sam smiled grimly. "You think you're so high-and-mighty, Mr. Killer, but you couldn't put down Sam Giancarlo. I'm still here, still free and on the streets because your government made a deal with me. Your government tells me, 'Old Sam, you talk for us and we forget everything you do.'" He laughed then. "I'm still kickin', bastard."

Bolan turned from him without a word and collected his weapons. He and Joan left all the rest behind, letting Old Sam take whatever measures he wished to dispose of the bodies all over his den.

They got in the Cougar and rode off down the street, passing a black Lincoln half a block farther on. Bolan was silent, remembering everything Old Sam had said to him, remembering the road that had brought him to this confrontation with the old man. "Still on the streets," he had said, "still kicking."

Bolan stopped the car in the lot of the convenience store where he'd bought the aspirin earlier that evening.

"What's up?" Meredith asked.

"Gotta make a call." Bolan strode toward the nearby pay phone.

A quarter got him a dial tone, and a quick call to information elicited the number he wanted. Then he dialed again and listened to ten rings at the other end before a voice answered, "Oklahoma City Police Department."

"Yeah," Bolan said. "Theft: auto."

Another line rang, a woman answering this time. "Don't say anything," Bolan told her, "just write this down. The auto theft ring is operating out of a chain of body shops called Lucky Sam's. The chain is owned by a man you know as Robert Pressman, but who is actually known as Old Sam Giancarlo, a Chicago mobster."

"What's your..."

"Never mind that." Bolan hung up and returned to the car feeling a lot better.

Bolan headed the Cougar toward the airport, all the while thinking about blood and heredity, about upbringing and conditioning. Laws were the rules of civilization, rules that helped us walk out of the jungle and learn to live together in peace. If man was ever to survive on this planet, the rule of law had to prevail over the rule of instinct, the killing urge.

The urge to kill.

The urge that kills.

Old Sam would live to testify against Ben Villani and his contacts, but at least now he'd be doing it from a cage, a place where animals are kept for the safety of others. To Mack Bolan, the Executioner, that made a big difference. For to him, crime wasn't a job or a gentleman's game run by situation ethics. It was a war, a nasty war for the highest stakes, a war in which there could be no mercy and no quarter.

**Adventure and suspense
in a treacherous new world**

JAMES AXLER
DEATH LANDS®
Dectra Chain

Ryan Cawdor and his band of postholocaust survivors become
caught up in a horrifying nightmare after they materialize in a
nineteenth-century Maine whaling village and Ryan is shang-
haied by a ferocious captain, who will go to any length to man
her whaling ship.

Mack Bolan's

PHOENIX FORCE

by Gar Wilson

The battle-hardened, five-man commando unit known as Phoenix Force continues its onslaught against the hard realities of global terrorism in an endless crusade for freedom, justice and the rights of the individual. Schooled in guerrilla warfare, equipped with the latest in lethal weapons, Phoenix Force's adventures have made them a legend in their own time. Phoenix Force is the free world's foreign legion!

"Gar Wilson is excellent! Raw action attacks the reader on every page."

—Don Pendleton

Phoenix Force titles are available wherever paperbacks are sold.

PF-1

You don't know what **NONSTOP HIGH-VOLTAGE ACTION** is until you've read your **4 FREE GOLD EAGLE NOVELS**